THE GOLEM

A Montague & Strong Detective Agency Novel

ORLANDO A. SANCHEZ

BITTEN PEACHES
PUBLISHING

Published by: Bitten Peaches Publishing

Cover Art: Deranged Doctor Design www.derangeddoctordesign.com

DESCRIPTION

It's uncomfortable between a rock and a hard place.

When the NYTF reports that a golem, a large rock creature, is terrorizing parts of the city and destroying hubs of power, Ezra calls on Montague & Strong to investigate and stop the creature.

Their first reaction is to refuse.

Except there's one problem.

No one refuses Ezra, a personification of Death, without grave consequences.

Now, Monty and Simon, together with Ursula of the DAMNED, must uncover how the golem was created and who would use it to destroy hubs of power, without being crushed in the process.

What they uncover, will have them face a power beyond their abilities and make choices with dire consequences.

Consequences they may not be ready for...yet.

"When you're stuck between a rock and a hard place, blow up the rock."—Uncle Dex

"What is misunderstood is feared, what is feared is eradicated. The supernatural and normal world can never co-exist without a veil between them. To think differently is foolish and naive; to work toward this end, self-destructive and fatal."—Connor Montague

ONE

Monty's phone rang as we drove downtown to meet Ezra. He handed me the keepsaker box as he reached for his phone. With the press of a button, he connected the call, sending it to the Dark Goat's Bluetooth system.

"*Prepodavatel*—teacher. You need to come to building. Now."

It was Olga. An agitated, angry-sounding Olga.

"What did she call you...*preposition*?" I asked under my breath. "She sounds heated for an ice-queen."

"Stronk," she said with her usual name-mangling. "Good, you are there. Bring Cece teacher to building—now. You have problem."

She ended the call abruptly.

"When she says, 'You have problem', she means the royal you, right?"

"I think she means any 'you' that doesn't include her. Turn us around. She sounded quite upset."

"You're concerned because she sounded upset?"

"Do you recall how you referred to Olga when she convinced me to take on Cecelia as an apprentice?"

"You mean when she threatened to deep-freeze The Moscow?"

"Yes. It was a subtle demonstration of her power."

"Subtle?" I asked with a shudder. "I remember her freezing most of the table without so much as an eyebrow wiggle."

"She doesn't seem the type to fluster easily," Monty said. "Anything that gets her disturbed warrants paying attention to."

"Disturbed sounds about right," I said with a nod. "I remember that convincing session. She turned her office into a fairly passable meat locker."

At the mention of the word *meat*, Peaches, who was snoring in the backseat in a mega-sprawl, opened an eye and perked an ear.

<Are we getting meat?>

<No. Is that all you listen for? Is that your entire focus —really?>

<Is there anything more important than meat?>

<We're going to the place soon. Go back to your nap.>

Peaches went from semi-alert to full-devour mode, including the drool.

<The place? Are we really? It's been so long since I've eaten. I'm so hungry.>

<I guess we're not going to count the several pounds of meat you ate an hour ago?>

<So long ago. An hour. I'm hungry. Will the old man have meat for me?>

I didn't bother answering because I knew where the conversation was headed. Monty cleared his throat to get my attention. He somehow always knew when I was "speaking" to Peaches. *Must be a mage thing.*

"You referred to her as the 'ice-queen building owner', which, in retrospect, seems to be quite accurate."

"You're saying she *is* the ice-queen?"

"Not *the* ice-queen, rather *an* ice-queen or dignitary," Monty answered. "I'm still waiting to hear back from my contacts at the Golden Circle. It does make sense, though, considering her level of power and the fact that she owns a substantial amount of prime real estate in this city."

"Which would require serious wealth."

"More importantly, considerable influence. No one who has approached her to sell has been successful. She must be connected to the Jotnar in some way, or they never would have entrusted Cecelia to her care."

"Olga doesn't seem like the type to fold under strong-arm tactics," I said, making a U-turn on the Westside Highway at 23rd Street. "To own The Moscow, and keep it —she's either a very effective business—woman, or dangerous. Or, more likely, both."

"Indeed. Which means we have a problem."

"You realize we're putting Ezra on the back—burner to address this problem with Olga," I said, stepping down on the accelerator.

"I'm afraid we don't have a choice," Monty said, glancing at me. "Ezra will have to wait. Hurry."

TWO

We were two blocks away from The Moscow when I felt the chill in the air.

"What the hell is that?" I asked with a shudder. "Feels like we just drove into the Arctic."

"I believe that is our problem," Monty answered, pointing ahead. "Not quite the Arctic, but close."

<It's the cold girl.>

<Excuse me?>

<The one who finds me beautiful. It smells like her.>

<You can smell this...? Really? I thought your sense of smell was set to meat and little else.>

<Her guardian smells better than meat from the place.>

I almost turned in surprise at this statement.

<Better than meat? Are you feeling okay? Not a sentence I ever expected to hear from you.>

<Can we go to the place now?>

<After we deal with this situation.>

"Stop the car," Monty said. "Bloody hell."

I stopped the Dark Goat about half a block away. My

eyes were registering the image, but my brain was having a hard time processing it. There was ice everywhere.

"Is that our building?"

"Yes. It would seem it has undergone some alterations."

"Alterations? We now live in the Fortress of Solitude. Are you telling me little Cece—?"

"Cecelia, apparently, is only little in stature, not power," Monty said. "This is a significant shift."

"Significant, how?"

"She is an ice mage from a Jotnar bloodline," Monty said, peering at The Moscow. "I didn't expect a shift of this magnitude for at least two or three decades."

"Decades? Are you saying she's going to get even stronger?"

"Quite," Monty said with a nod. "Jotnar ice mages can achieve Archmage levels early. I just didn't expect it this soon."

"Are you telling me Cece is an Archmage?"

"No, don't be daft. If she were at that level of power and lost control, the building and most of the surrounding area, would have been reduced to rubble, and Olga would be hunting us down."

"Not a scenario I want to visit, thanks," I said, admiring the Arctic wasteland forming around us. "She's doing this from inside the building?"

"Yes," Monty answered. "It seems her ability has targeted the moisture in the air. We need to get to her. If she's shifting, this will get worse before it gets better."

"Worse, really? I think we've skated past worse long ago. See what I did there?"

"Ice metaphors—droll," Monty said, exiting the Dark

Goat and forming a flame orb. "Your wit never ceases to disappoint."

"Thank you—I think?"

"This has escalated considerably," Monty said, looking around. "How are you with extreme cold?"

"How extreme?"

"Think Arctic in the winter."

"I don't make a habit of visiting the Arctic, winter or otherwise, and I left my parka in the icicle we call our home. I'm going to go with: I freeze my ass off in extreme cold?"

Monty nodded. "I assumed your curse would offer some measure of protection," he said, gesturing. Small orbs of flame floated in my direction, enveloping me in a cocoon of warmth. "That should keep you homeostatic."

"Homo what?"

"Homeo—never mind. It will keep you warm and comfortable."

"Why would you assume my curse would keep me warm? It deals with damage, not temperature."

"What do you think happens to unprotected skin in sub-zero temperatures?"

"Oh," I said with the dawning realization of imminent death. "Hell."

"Not unless it's frozen over. Let's go."

I stepped out of the Dark Goat and peered down the street. The lower floors of The Moscow, including the lobby, were encased in thick, softly glowing blue ice. The sidewalk and street surrounding the entrance had been converted into one large sheet of that same ice.

"How did she—?"

"We have a more immediate concern," Monty said,

pulling on a sleeve. I could sense him gathering energy as we walked down the street. "Make sure your creature remains calm."

"Why would he need to remain calm?" I asked, then saw who was standing in front of the building. "Oh."

"Yes," Monty answered. "Let's not escalate this situation."

Standing in front of the building with arms crossed, glaring at us as we approached, was a very displeased Olga.

<Do not attack the ice lady in front of the building.>

<She smells like the cold girl.>

<She's very angry right now with Monty.>

<Why? Is she hungry?>

<She feels we have something to do with the ice.>

<It's the cold girl, not the angry man.>

<I know, but he's responsible for her using her ability properly.>

<She's the cold girl.>

<Yes, she's an ice mage.>

<The building is cold now. She is using her ability properly.>

I couldn't disagree with the logic.

<She's not supposed to make the building cold. That's why the ice lady is upset. She doesn't want her building covered in ice.>

<Maybe you should take her to the place. Meat will make her happy.>

<I don't think it's that easy. Just stay close, boy. This can go sideways, fast.>

<Why would we go sideways? I can't walk sideways.>

<Make sure you don't attack, unless I say so.>

<Do you want me to attack sideways?>

<No attacking in any direction unless I tell you to.>

<You sound hungry. Maybe you should eat some meat?>

I shook my head with a sigh and focused on Monty, ignoring my single-minded hellhound.

"So, we're trying diplomacy again?" I asked.

"Olga is formidable. I'd rather not have to face her in battle. Tact and diplomacy are always our first options."

"If that fails?" I asked. "Not that it will, I'm just thinking about all the other times we tried to be diplomatic. Our success rate sucks."

"Let me do the talking. It may be safer if you and your creature stay back a safe distance."

"Safe distance? Like Queens?"

"This is why you should stay back. She doesn't seem to be in the mood for your acerbic wit."

"Her loss," I said, letting Monty continue ahead, but keeping somewhat close. "This isn't your fault, by the way. How could you have known Cece was a super ice mage?"

"She's my apprentice," Monty said under his breath. "Everything she does is my responsibility."

"Can you take Olga?" I asked, making sure my mala bracelet and Grim Whisper were accessible. "Is she that much of a threat?"

"Let's not find out."

"She's that strong?"

"Stronger."

THREE

"Do you see building?" Olga asked, glaring ice daggers at Monty and waving an arm in the direction of The Moscow. "Ice everywhere. I said no damage to building. This. Is. Big. Damage."

I felt that was something of an obvious statement, but kept my opinion to myself. I noticed Andrei, our doorman, and the valet who used to park our cars, were nowhere to be seen. I hoped they weren't trapped in the ice.

"Are you certain this was caused by Cecelia?" Monty asked. "This level of power is quite extraordinary for a child."

"She is only ice mage inside building. Now building and street full of ice. This"—Olga pointed at The Moscow—"is your student. You fix, now."

Olga stepped back from the entrance, giving Monty access. I stepped close to him, allowing Olga some space in case she felt the need to unleash some icicles of death at us. She gave me the same glacial look of potential pain she'd shared with Monty.

"She is not a happy camper," I said under my breath, glancing her way. "I've never seen her this pissed."

"Judging from the extent of the encasing," Monty said, narrowing his eyes and examining the ice, "I can only assume the garage is completely filled with ice. It appears to have traveled downward before ascending."

"Can you undo this?" I asked Monty when we had stepped away from Olga. "She's an ice dignitary, so why can't she remove the ice?"

Monty stepped up to the ice encasing the building. The soft blue glow pulsed with energy.

"This isn't normal ice," he said, placing a hand on its surface. "It's imbued with substantial energy."

"Really, what gave it away? The fact that it's surrounding our building, or that it's glowing?"

"Actually, it's the energy signature," Monty answered. "I don't think Olga wants to tangle with this kind of power."

"Is that because she can't, or won't?"

"The latter. The energy structure beneath the ice is unstable. If undone incorrectly, it could destroy the structural integrity of the building, causing a catastrophic chain reaction within the interior of the edifice."

"That definitely falls into the damage category. Which means an angrier Olga. Any way could we prevent that? I like living here."

"As do I. I'm trying to ascertain the extent of the current damage without causing a collapse—not as easy as it appears."

"Can't you throw up some 'runes of building support or structural reinforcement' to prevent the collapse?"

"Battlemagic has a tendency to lean more toward the destructive, not constructive, side of the spectrum. This is similar to unraveling a tangled web. The wrong cast from the outside can set off the ice and topple—"

"The building, which is currently full of people," I finished, looking at the ice.

"A building which cannot be presently evacuated."

"Why can't we get them out? I'll call Ramirez, and we can evac—"

The sound of ice cracking shot through the night. I saw more blue ice had formed and crept up the side of the building.

"Bringing the NYTF here will only put them in danger," Monty answered, gesturing. A group of white runes floated into the ice and disappeared. "We don't have that kind of time."

"Well, unless you have some kind of industrial blowtorch or an instant melt rune, this is going to get worse."

I looked at the ice slowly rising up the side of the building.

"We need to get inside and address this at the source," Monty said, following my gaze upward. "The sooner, the better."

"We can just teleport—"

Monty shook his head.

"Too dangerous. My teleportation circle could create runic backlash. We need to be subtle about how we enter the space."

"What about Peaches?" I asked, pointing at my hellhound.

"I said subtle," Monty said, glancing at Peaches. "Your creature is about as subtle as a battering ram."

"True, but he *can* step in-between without a circle. Is that subtle enough to not set off the ice?"

Monty looked at Peaches, who gave him a low rumble in response.

"It could work," Monty said after a pause. "Planewalking is similar to teleportation. He'd have to be able to bring me with him; that way, I can assess the extent of the damage and cast a reversal before the entire structure is buried under ice."

"Will you be able to stop her?" I asked, looking at all the ice around us. "Cece is just a little girl, but she's pretty strong."

"We don't have much of a choice," Monty said, stepping back from the ice. "If we don't stop her, the building is in danger, and so are we."

"From the falling debris?"

"From an angry Olga."

"Good point," I said, glancing back at the still-glaring Olga. "I think I'd prefer the falling building than dealing with her."

"Wise choice. See if your creature can pinpoint Cecelia's location. If he can, he needs to take me—"

"Us," I interrupted. "Take *us*."

Monty raised an eyebrow.

"Is he able to take both of us?" Monty asked. "That may strain his abilities."

"We'll find out, but I'm not staying out here with the angry ice queen."

"Ask him now. We're running out of time."

FOUR

<Hey, boy, can you smell where Cece—the cold girl is?>

<Yes, but she smells different.>

<Different how?>

<She smells...more.>

<That's not very helpful. Do you think you can take us to her?
>

<You are my bondmate. I can take you anywhere. The angry man will have to hold on if we go in-between.>

I was about to inform Monty of our hellhound travel arrangements, when I heard the screech of tires behind us. I turned to see a 1966 orange VW Type-2 bus slide into the large ice sheet surrounding The Moscow, then slam into the Dark Goat with a crash. The grating sound of metal on metal filled the street as the bus slid off the Dark Goat.

The driver tried unsuccessfully to correct the slide. He overcompensated, turning the wheel in the opposite direction, causing the bus to fishtail and hit the Dark Goat again, before gaining some measure of control. A few seconds later, he skidded to a stop on the ice.

I drew Grim Whisper.

"What are you doing?" Monty asked.

"Shooting the driver who just slammed into the Dark Goat. That's what I'm doing."

"Put that away," Monty hissed. "We both know the car suffered no damage."

"Won't be able to say the same thing for the driver. Besides, I'm carrying persuaders. It will only be excruciating, not lethal."

Two men stepped out of the VW bus and approached The Moscow.

"We have more pressing concerns to attend to," Monty said. "Shooting bystanders will only complicate matters further."

"It's the principle of the thing. No one slams into the Dark Goat. Where the hell did he learn how to drive?"

"Probably not New York," Monty said, turning back to the building. "We have a frozen building to deal with. Let it go."

"Oi," the taller of the two men said, pointing over his shoulder with a thumb when they were closer. "Is that your vehicle back there?"

"You mean the vehicle *you* slammed into with your pumpkinmobile—twice?"

"Yes. Where did you learn to park? Your beast of a vehicle is blocking the road. We're holding you liable for any damage to our bus."

"You're holding *us* liable?" I asked as I turned my head slowly to Monty, giving him the *can I shoot them now?* look. Monty shook his head. "Liable for what? *You* hit my car."

"This is official business," Tall and Bald said. I recognized the accent as from Monty's part of the world. "You are actively hindering an investigation."

I unleashed a glare that easily hit a four on the Eastwood glare-o-meter.

"Excuse me?" I asked, completely confused. "Who are you?"

"Robert Bangers," Tall and Bald said, and pointed to the shorter man next to him, "and my associate, Steven Mash. Bangers and Mash—Paranormal Investigators of the Arcane.""

"Who did you say you were again?" I asked as Monty took a breath, probably counting to one hundred to keep from unleashing an orb of destruction at the pair. "I didn't get your names?"

"We have this situation under control," Tall and Bald said while he pushed up his glasses on the bridge of his nose, looking at Monty and me. "I suggest you two,"—he glanced down at Peaches—"umm...three...get somewhere safe. This can get dangerous."

They answered my initial question more directly by reaching into their jackets, almost causing me to perforate them, before retrieving their wallets and flashing badges at us. I looked over at Steven who gave me a bro nod of recognition. He was significantly shorter than Bangers, but I could tell by the fit of his clothing, that he trained. He had an ex-military look to him and figured he was the brawn to Bangers' brains.

"You can't possibly be serious," Monty said. "Bangers and Mash? Really?"

"Rolls off the tongue, doesn't it?" Bangers said with a smile. "I thought up the name."

"Quite...creative," Monty said after a pause. "Why are you here?"

"We picked up some strange energy signatures—well Robert did—and we headed right over," Steven said, glancing at Bangers. "We have experience with these kinds of situations."

"Do you, now?" Monty asked, turning to Bangers. "What's your assessment here?"

Bangers looked over at Mash as if to say, *these poor noobs are clearly out of their depth*, and took a step closer to the ice.

"Clearly, this is the work of an ice demon," Bangers said, his voice grim. "The ice surrounding the location of this building indicates that it rests on a cold ley line. This positioning attracted the ice demon entity to unleash its power on the building and surrounding area."

"Ice demon?" I asked. "Really?"

"Pretty clear when you know what to look for," Bangers answered. "You'd be safer over there"—he pointed across the street—"out of the line of fire. No telling how this demon will react once we breach."

"We can't be responsible for your safety," Mash said, nodding. "This is a professional investigation."

I glanced over at Olga, who looked ready to freeze Bangers and Mash on the spot and shatter them into little Professional Paranormal Investigator ice cubes.

"Monty?" I looked over at him, and then looked over at Olga. "You may want to have a word."

"Indeed," he said, looking at Bangers and Mash. "Keep this conversation here."

Monty walked off in Olga's direction as I holstered Grim Whisper.

"You've been doing this a long time, then?" I asked, focusing on Bangers.

"Ever since I left the Golden Circle—"

"Golden Circle?" I asked, trying very hard to keep a straight face. "The mage sect? That Golden Circle?"

"Yes, I'm surprised you've heard of it," Bangers said, raising an eyebrow.

"You're a mage?"

"Yes, I am," Bangers said. "What do you know of the Golden Circle?"

"Not much—rumors and stories. It's supposed to be one of the strongest—"

"It's the most powerful sect of mages that still teaches battlemagic."

"Battlemagic—wow."

"I wouldn't expect you to understand, you not being a mage and all."

Peaches rumbled next to my leg. I patted his head as Bangers looked down at my hellhound.

"Is your dog trained?" Bangers asked. "Would hate to see it harmed while we undergo our mission."

"Your mission? Oh, right. The ice demon," I said. "You don't have to worry about Peaches"—I rubbed his massive head—"he's very well trained. We'll stay out of your way. This looks like mage business."

"Peaches...really?" Bangers asked, looking at my hellhound. "Well, it's good to see some non-mages understand the delicate nature and severity of our work."

"You're right, I'm not a mage," I said. "You plan on using some of this 'battlemagic' to stop the ice demon?"

"Only thing that can work in this situation," Bangers answered. "Clearly, this is an attack on the building. My associate here"—he glanced at Mash—"is an ex-Navy Seal. Trust me when I say we're prepared."

"Ex-Navy Seal? Impressive. Which team?"

"Classified," Mash answered. "I'm not at liberty to divulge that information."

"Totally understand, sensitive information and all," I said with a nod. "Probably safer that way."

"You have no idea," Mash said. "We've seen and done things most civilians wouldn't understand, much less believe."

"You do sound equipped and prepared," I said. "I'm just surprised I've never heard of your team. Are you new to the city?"

"We go where we're needed," Mash said. "Right now, this city is in need of our services."

"Not surprising," Bangers said, with a self-important sniff. "Investigators of our caliber don't exactly take out ads in the paper. What do you think we are —wizards?"

"Good point," I said. "You seem like a top-notch team. How are you going in, if you don't mind sharing with an amateur like me?"

"We plan on using our patented Bangersmash," Bangers said with a hint of pride. "It's very effective in these situations."

"Let me guess. You created that name, too."

"I did," Bangers answered smugly. "In terms you can understand: we are going to use large amounts of explosives to blow an enormous hole in the ice. Then, we go in and subdue the ice demon. It's quite complicated. I don't think you could understand all of the intricacies of mage work."

"Sounds complicated, but it looks like you're ready to deal with it."

"We are. Now, please step back and leave this to the professionals."

I stepped back as Bangers headed back to their pumpkin bus, which was also surprisingly unscathed from its crash into the Dark Goat. Mash trailed behind him.

Monty returned from speaking with Olga who, amazingly, looked even more upset than she had before the arrival of Bangers and Mash.

"She suggested deep freezing the pair along with their vehicle, then dropping them in the river," Monty said when he drew close. "I advised her that wasn't a prudent course of action."

I glanced over at Olga.

"You told her you didn't know them, right?" I asked. "I only ask because she looks like she doesn't want to follow your advice."

"She will refrain from freezing them for now, but we must act."

"Are you going to let them go in?"

"Bangers and Mash?" Monty asked. "Only if I want to have the building destroyed. I don't understand how they've survived this long."

"Says he trained at the Golden Circle—your sect."

"Impossible," Monty snapped. "His energy signature is nearly undetectable. If he's a mage of the Golden Circle, then I'm the Ultimate Grand Archmage of the Universe."

"Not a mage, I'm guessing."

"Precisely. The child in this building, who caused this ice dwarfs his ability by orders of magnitude."

"Well, if the other one is an ex-Navy Seal, I'm Delta

Force, CIA, and MI6 all at once," I said. "I do like the name, though. For some reason Bangers and Mash makes me hungry. Kind of rolls off the tongue."

Monty just stared at me for a few long seconds before shaking his head.

"Bangers was never at the Golden Circle, and like you, I doubt his associate is an ex-Navy anything."

"The real question is: how does he know about the Golden Circle?"

"And how did they sense the energy signature of The Moscow?"

"Bangers could be sensitive. That doesn't make him a mage. It does make him dangerous."

"He has a unique method of breaching the building, something called the Bangersmash. It involves lots of explosives. At least he has the mage mentality."

"Hilarious," Monty said. "I think Bangers and Mash need to be introduced to the concept of early retirement before they hurt themselves."

"More like before Olga hurts them."

"That, too. Here they come."

I turned to see the pair approaching with a large military ordnance case carried between them.

"If they open that case, this won't end well," I said. "Before you blast them to bits...let's try diplomacy."

FIVE

Monty stepped forward and intercepted Bangers and Mash before they could get close to the building.

"It would be an excellent learning opportunity if you allowed us, who are clearly not on your level of power or experience, to deal with this situation," Monty said in his calmest voice ever, which was somehow scarier than his usual voice of menace. "You would do us a great honor."

"Please step aside," Bangers said, as he and Mash put down the large case. "We don't want any of you getting hurt. Mash, retrieve the C4 and begin placing charges around the entrance."

"Since we've both studied at the Golden Circle, I'm sure you're familiar with the Rule of Hierarchy," Monty said. "It's quite the tradition."

"You studied at the Golden Circle?" Bangers asked, his voice cracking slightly."You're a mage?"

"Evidently not on your level of power, since I don't recall ever seeing or hearing of you during my studies there. They must have kept you separated away with the gifted mages."

"They must have," Bangers barely managed to squeak.

"In any case," Monty said, waving the words away. "That is where I learned the Rule of Hierarchy, which I'm sure you're familiar with, yes?"

"The Rule of Hierarchy?" Bangers asked. "Oh, of course. There were many rules at the Circle."

"I'm sure you recall this one," Monty continued. "The one that states that a higher-level mage must allow a lower-level mage to commence the operations on any serious mission to minimize the danger to the senior?"

"That Rule of Hierarchy—yes...yes, I recall it very well," Bangers said nervously. "I don't see how that applies here, though. Clearly, I'm the only mage in the—"

Monty gestured, forming a blinding white orb of energy in his hand. Bangers and Mash both looked on in awe, before stepping back several feet, away from Monty.

"It's clear, seeing as how you're the senior in this case, according to the rule, that you are obligated to allow me to attempt to get this situation under control first."

"Now...now, that I recall the rule better," Bangers said, his voice tight, and his eyes fixed on the orb. "I think you're right. You and your associate should try to get this situation handled. Mash and I will be near our vehicle, for when inevitably, you need our assistance."

"Inevitably," Monty answered, absorbing the orb. "Thank you so much for this opportunity, and I agree—I think you would be safest if you would remain close to your vehicle for the duration of this process."

Bangers and Mash picked up the case and moved as quickly as possible to the VW Pumpkin.

"Who is that?" I heard Mash ask. "How did he do that?"

"He's a mage from the Golden Circle," Bangers answered hurriedly. "Let's get back to the bus."

"Wait, *the* Golden Circle?" Mash said, glancing our way. "He's a *real* mage? You said we wouldn't run into any real mages."

"I was wrong. Now shut it until we get to the bus."

"That was generous of you," I said, watching Bangers and Mash head back to their Pumpkin. "Rule of Hierarchy? Not bad. I'm guessing there's no such rule?"

"Of course not," Monty said. "I know the type. This gave him a way to save face and clear the area."

Olga stepped to where we stood.

"You go now," she said. "Before building breaks."

It wasn't a request.

"If those two return while we are inside, stop them," Monty said, "but don't kill them."

Olga nodded and crossed her arms.

<We're ready, boy.>

<The angry man has to hold on.>

"Peaches says you have to hold on."

Monty knelt and wrapped an arm around Peaches' neck.

"I'm ready," Monty said, looking down at Peaches. "Inform your creature to keep his salivation to a minimum."

<Don't drool on Monty. He doesn't like saliva on his clothes.>

<Can he make some meat when we get inside?>

<I'll ask him once we get inside. If you don't drool on him, he'll probably do it.>

Peaches gave a low rumble as the runes along his flanks

shone with violet light. With a low bark, the building disappeared.

SIX

I don't know how long we spent in-between.

Planewalking was slightly different from teleportation. Whenever Monty cast a teleportation circle, the effect was instantaneous. I stepped into the circle and arrived wherever we needed to moments later.

It took my body several minutes to understand the process, which caused me excruciating agony. Planewalking with Peaches was closer to sitting in the longest, most insane roller coaster in the world without a harness, seatbelt, or any other method of staying attached to said rollercoaster, to say nothing of the agony that came after it was over.

We arrived in the hallway outside our space. Everything was covered in the same blue, glowing ice. I leaned against the wall and waited for the rest of my stomach to catch up with me.

"Inter-planar travel should be getting easier for you," Monty said, patting Peaches on the head. "Good hellhound."

Peaches answered with a rumble and a body shake, which nearly bounced me off the wall with a shattered spine.

"I think we have different definitions for *easier*," I said, waiting for the hallway to stop twisting. "The intestines I left outside would disagree about this getting easier in any way, shape, or form."

"If you'd stop fighting your bonds," Monty said, narrowing his eyes at me, "you wouldn't suffer this way."

I took a step off the wall, felt the floor tilt, and thought better of it, leaning back until everything stopped moving.

"I'm not fighting my bonds," I said. "I'm just adjusting to them."

"Your adjusting needs adjusting," Monty said, looking down the hallway to our door. "Can you move? We don't have the luxury of relaxing."

"Relaxing?" I asked with a groan. "Is that what I'm doing?"

"You certainly aren't addressing the situation at hand," Monty said, looking at the door where Cece lived. "Jotnar ice mage? Pressed for time? Imminent building collapse? Seething ice-queen landlord? Any of those ring a bell?"

"No need to be pushy," I said. "It's not like my internal organs are convulsing in agony, making anything but shallow breathing an accomplishment."

"If you stop fighting your bonds, this won't be an issue," Monty answered with a total lack of compassion. "It's not complicated. Embrace who you are."

"I think Hallmark is looking for some compassion writers—you'd fit right in."

"I don't do compassion," he said. "Mages are pragmatists. We see the situation as it is, not as we wish it to be. You need to do the same, sooner rather than later."

I stared at him. He was right, but I would never tell him that.

"I've just gotten used to the idea of Ebonsoul floating around inside of me somewhere," I answered, straightening myself out. "Let's take this one step at a time."

"You may not have the luxury of time," Monty said, looking down the hallway at Cece's door. "Haven't you noticed the caliber of your enemies? They seem to be getting stronger, commensurate with the increase in your power."

"*My* enemies?" I asked. "I'm not the mage—you are."

"A valid point."

"Exactly," I said, feeling somewhat vindicated. "You are the one dealing with all the energy slinging and runic manipulation."

"However," he began, "Kali cursed *you*—Chosen One. Hades gave *you* a hellhound to bond with. It also seemed like Chaos was particularly focused on *you* for some reason."

"That was all because of a mage—"

"You also happen to be energetically intertwined with an ancient vampire, whose mental stability is...questionable at best. You recently ingested dragon blood and survived, faced the guardian of the Underworld, and regularly have conversations with an agent of causality."

"It's mostly your fault, you know."

"I disagree. Until you embrace who you are," he said, pointing a finger at me, "and accept responsibility for *your* part in *your* life, you will experience runic dissonance, which is expressed in rather interesting ways—like having your internal organs convulsing in pain every time you teleport or planewalk."

"I don't know which is worse: the lecture or the agony of planewalking," I said, upset. Mostly at myself, because his words contained enough truth to sting. "Are you done?"

He let out a short sigh and shook his head.

"The list *is* quite long," Monty said, nodding. "I'd continue, but as I mentioned, we are pressed for time."

"Seriously?"

"I'm a Montague and a mage. I'm always serious."

"You know, ever since we met, my life has been radically altered."

"For the better," Monty said with a nod. "I agree. Now shall we address this current situation, which, surprisingly, is not of your making?"

"After you," I said, pointing at Cece's door. "She's your apprentice, Darth Monty."

"Not only is that inaccurate, it's not remotely humorous," Monty said, approaching Cece's door. "She is my *student*. While the terminology is correct, the context is wrong. She has not 'gone over' to the dark side, nor am I a Sith Lord."

"Freezing a building full of people, with the potential of reducing it to a pile of rubble, sounds pretty dark side to me."

"If it were intentional," Monty said, gesturing and forming several large, white-hot orbs in front of her door. "Then I could see this act as being dark. As it stands, she's probably scared witless at her shift."

"Oh, this is what Jotnar fear looks like?" I asked. "I'd hate to see her angry, determined, and focused."

"Yes, you would," Monty said his voice grim. "The

Jotnar are staggeringly powerful, their ice mages in particular. This is most likely Cecelia losing control because of the shift."

"Wait—should we be going in there if she's out of control?" I asked. "I mean, I seem to recall your last shift was dangerous...mostly for me."

"We don't have a choice," Monty said, extending his arm. "We can't stop her from out here."

"Oh, hell," I said, pressing the main bead on my mala bracelet and pulling up my shield. I made sure Peaches was behind the shield. "I hope you know what you're doing."

"So do I," he said. "I've never dealt with a Jotnar shift."

Monty gestured again, forming another shield in front of mine as the orbs floated into the door with a loud hiss.

A moment later, the door exploded.

SEVEN

Chunks of ice, wood, and metal lay scattered all over the hallway. The door leading to Cece's place was gone, replaced by a gaping hole. Monty stepped in through the jagged opening that used to be the door.

"Bloody hell," I heard him curse under his breath. "This is incredible."

"You mean the ice everywhere?" I asked, dropping my shield and following him in a second later. "Or the fact that this was done by a little girl?"

"Both."

We were standing in what I assumed was the foyer. It was hard to tell, since everything had the feel of an arctic ice cave. The space was laid out similarly to ours, with some distinct differences. The short foyer led to a large room; we had turned ours into a reception area for clients, but in Cece's space, it was a large living room. Off this room was the kitchen, and another hallway, which I guessed led to a bedroom.

Our space was substantially larger, missing a few walls,

and I hoped lacked the additional architectural feature of magic ice. We had the same hallway which led back to the sleeping quarters. In our space, we also had the conference room, and the additional door that led to Uncle Dex's room, which was best left unopened.

There was ice everywhere. In the background, I could hear the sound of distant wind blowing.

"That sound. Is that—?"

"Cecelia, yes. That sound would be the location of the source we need."

"A question," I said, looking around. "The ice, is everywhere on the floor at this point, does this mean our place is currently a winter wonderland?"

"No," Monty said, stepping farther into the space. "Cecelia is powerful, but the defenses on our space are considerably stronger."

"That's reassuring," I said. "I'd hate to have all my things frozen."

"This isn't typical ice," Monty said, looking around a corner. "Once it's dispelled, no water will be left behind."

"Do you know a dry ice dispelling rune that can handle that?"

"Let me clarify," Monty said. "Once Cecelia dispels the ice, there will be no water residue."

"You can't do it?"

"No. Remember, we want to keep the building intact. If I attempt to remove this ice, it can result in a collapse, with us inside of it."

"In that case, we'd better let her do it, then," I said. "Do you think she will listen?"

"Hard to tell. It depends on how deep into this shift she is."

"I'd say she's in pretty deep," I said, taking in the surrounding ice. "Can you sense where she is?"

"No need," Monty answered and pointed to a closed door. "Over there."

"I'll take the runically enhanced ice storm behind door number one," I said, staying back just in case the door flew off its hinges. "That doesn't look good."

I realized the temperature had dropped when our exhalations formed little clouds that quickly crystallized into ice, falling to the floor. The door was forcibly vibrating, and the sound of the wind had increased from stiff breeze to approaching hurricane.

Lying still in front of the door was Rags, Cece's guardian. I focused on Rags' body first, dreading the worst, until I saw her flank slowly rise and fall with each breath. Around her, ice and blue energy swirled as the intensity of the wind rose and fell. Frost was slowly forming on and around her body.

"It's worse than I thought," Monty muttered under his breath. "We need containment."

"I'm guessing the gale of destruction is the source of the ice?"

"Yes and no," Monty said over the whine of wind. "Cecelia is the source; the storm raging around her is an expression of her shift."

"I'm not going to enjoy the next words you're going to say, am I?"

"We need to open that door."

"I was right. We need to move her guardian first."

"Agreed. Her guardian needs assistance," Monty said over the rising whine of wind. "Have your creature take her outside. She can't help in that state. I'll begin the cast to get us inside."

Peaches let out a low rumble finishing with a soft whine.

<Boy, can you take—?>

<Yes!>

<You don't even know what I'm going to ask.>

<You want me to take the cold girl's guardian outside. I can.>

<I keep forgetting you can understand me.>

<I'm a hellhound. My level of understanding is elevators.>

<You mean elevated.>

<Can I use my saliva to heal her? She looks hurt.>

<Let's hold off on the magic drool for now. We don't know why she's in that state. Your saliva might make things worse.>

<My saliva can never make things worse. It has healing properties.>

<Once we know it's safe, you can use your saliva and drool on her. Until then, wait.>

<She's waiting for me to rescue her.>

<Don't think so, boy. I suggest not starting your next conversation by explaining how you came to her rescue.>

<Why not?>

<Trust me on this one. Powerful vampires—I mean, powerful females don't need to be rescued.>

<Should I start my conversation with meat? Everyone loves meat. I'm sure she likes meat.>

<Maybe just let her know you helped her keep the cold girl safe. She is a guardian, after all. She'd probably like that.>

<That makes sense. Not as good as meat, but good. Can I get her now?>

<Don't get too close to the door, and take her outside.>

<Can I have extra meat at the place once I rescue her?>

<You're asking now?>

<Frank says I need to do things for a living wage. He says I need to form an onion.>

<Frank needs to keep his radical ideas to himself. Once we're done with this situation, you and I are heading downtown to have a word with that lizard.>

<Dragon. Frank is a dragon.>

<Frank is going to be extinct when I finish with him.>

<Can I form an onion?>

<He meant union, and no, you can't form a union of one hellhound. Are you going to keep Rags waiting?>

<No, but meat is important.>

<I know. Meat is life. I'll make sure to speak to Ezra once we get to the place.>

<Thank you. Frank says negotiations under a dress are the best kind.>

<It's duress, and that's what Frank is going to feel when I see him. Once you get near her, blink out.>

<What do my eyes have to do with walking in-between?>

<That's what I call—never mind, go take her outside. Now, boy.>

Peaches padded down the hallway to where Rags lay. If the wind was affecting him, he gave no indication. It wasn't until he was closer, that I saw him square his body and dig into the ice covered floor to stop from slipping.

His massive paws dropped an inch into the ice as he fought the energy of the wind with each step. He gently placed a paw on Rags' side as the runes along his flanks blazed with red energy.

With a low bark that shook some of the ice, Peaches and Rags were gone.

EIGHT

Monty gestured and formed a lattice of violet energy that filled the hallway behind us.

"Monty, why is the lattice behind us?" I asked. "Wouldn't it be safer to place the lattice in front of us?"

"No, we need to open the door, and once we do"—he extended an arm down the hallway—"we can't let anything escape this containment area."

I glanced at the ice covering everything.

"I'd say we're past that point, considering we're currently standing in Siberia," I said. "What is there to contain? The ice is outside of the room."

"You're not paying attention," Monty said. "The ice is an expression of Cecelia's shift. Think of it as a side-effect. The real danger is Cecelia."

"Wonderful," I said. "We have to stop her without harming her. Any ideas?"

"Working on it," Monty said. "There's no precedent in my studies for Jotnar ice mage shifts of power."

The building started to creak as cracking sounds echoed throughout the hallway.

"Great, we get to die in a frozen wasteland in the middle of the city as you figure this out," I said as more creaking filled the hallway. "What the hell is that?"

"That would be the ice compromising the structural integrity of the building," Monty answered, focused on the door. "Now, unless you have any illuminating ideas on how to deal with this ice, let me concentrate."

"Maybe we should call Bangers and Mash?" I asked, not being able to resist. "I'm sure a few well-placed charges of C4—"

"Suggest those two again and I'll blast you myself."

I raised my hands in surrender and smiled.

"No need to get touchy. We do need to come up with a signature move, though. How about the Triple M?"

"The what?" Monty asked, gesturing and creating symbols in the air. "What is a Triple M?"

"The Massive Montague Maelstrom: Triple M. Guaranteed to bring the house down, well, building in this case. What do you think?"

"I think you should stop talking and prepare your shield—now."

"Maybe we'll just call it the MMM?"

"Would you prefer to remain out here while I go and try to subdue our Jotnar ice mage?"

"*Our*? She's your apprentice, O Darth Monty."

"Not...even...remotely...funny," Monty said, unleashing a barrage of small golden orbs at the door. "Brace yourself."

The enso pendant around my neck flared with violet light.

I pressed the bead on my mala bracelet, formed my shield again as the door blasted open. Wind and ice punched into us. Several long icicles of glowing magic ice embedded themselves in my shield, and a few more buried themselves in the walls, floor, and ceiling.

The ice that passed us crashed into the lattice and disappeared.

"You want to walk into that?" I asked, raising my voice over the wind. "That looks fairly lethal."

"One second," Monty said, flexing his jaw as he gestured again. "I will create an opening. When I do, we run in. Ready?"

"Not really," I said, shaking my head. "Maybe we should call your uncle?"

"Good idea," Monty said, forming a large violet orb laced with golden energy racing across its surface. "But we don't have that kind of time. Get ready!"

Monty unleashed the large, violet and golden orb at the door. It raced down the hallway and then began to slow.

"Is it supposed to do that?" I asked as the orb slowed to a near standstill. "Do you need to go give it a push?"

"Figuratively speaking, yes." Monty stepped close and placed a hand around the enso pendant. "This should do."

He outstretched his other arm and fired a column of violet energy at the large orb. For a few seconds, nothing happened. The orb swelled with energy, then sped past the threshold and into the ice storm.

The storm raged for a few moments, intensifying, and then suddenly stopped.

"Now! Run!" Monty yelled, taking off at speed toward the ice-storm door. "We won't have much time."

We stepped inside the ice-storm room. Monty cast

another lattice, sealing the entrance behind us. This room wasn't covered in ice, but a thick, blue fog obscured visibility.

"Do you see her?" I asked under my breath as I strained to see. "This fog makes it impossible to sense anything."

"Her presence is here, but I can't pinpoint her location. I fear this room is very much like Dex's room in our space."

"She's hiding?"

"Not necessarily," Monty said. "She's masking her signature to the point that she doesn't exist."

"That's called hiding. I can't sense her in here."

"It's more like camouflage...even you can do it, if you focused and controlled your breathing. It's only a matter of blending your signature frequency with your surroundings."

"Camouflage, another word for hiding—in plain sight."

"Humans are interacting waves, not physical beings," Monty started, obviously in an attempt to melt my brain. "Waves cannot be separated, which means you are connected to everything. If you can attune your frequency to your surroundings, you can effectively disappear."

"So, what you're saying is...I am one with the force and the force is with me?"

"I get the impression you were dropped on your head often when you were a child," Monty snapped. "It's the only thing that can explain that much trauma and idiocy."

"It's a gift," I said with a mock bow. "Your Zillerfied explanation doesn't help us find Cece, no matter what frequency she's on."

He shook his head. "I have to say the size of this

dimension is impressive. I underestimated her skill and ability."

"This is one of those time and relative dimensions in space situations, where it's bigger on the inside—great. This place could be enormous. It'll take forever to find her."

"She would have created something she knows, even unconsciously."

"This place does look vaguely familiar, like the cave we visited when we got the runic neutralizer."

"That's it. Her shift must have created a pocket dimension shaped after the Jotnar home," Monty said, turning slowly. "This is quite extraordinary. Her ability, even inadvertently, easily classifies her as a few shifts away from Archmage."

"I'm really glad you're impressed," I said. "Can we focus on finding Cece and stopping this before we're buried in The Moscow, along with everyone else in the building?"

"Good point," Monty said with a nod. "Let me see if a tracking rune will—"

"Welcome to your death, mage," a voice boomed around us.

"I think we found her," I said. "Seems like she wants a word—with you. It's strange, as I don't remember little Cece sounding like James Earl Jones. Maybe she has a cold —you know, all this ice."

"That's not Cecelia," Monty said, turning in the direction of the voice. "Not entirely. I should've expected this."

"You should've expected Cece to sound like an older, middle-aged man? What do you mean, not entirely?"

"The Jotnar are connected to an ancient consciousness,

it serves almost as a hive mind," Monty said. "It's usually dormant, surfacing only during times of extreme stress or danger."

"I'm guessing an ice mage shift qualifies as extreme stress and danger?"

"You will die today, Tristan Montague," the voice said. "For your transgression against my people. Your vow remains unfulfilled."

"There is no vow," Monty said with an edge to his voice. "There never was."

"Do you want me to wait outside?" I asked. "This sounds personal."

"Stop talking," Monty answered. "I highly doubt it's just me this entity is focused on."

"For befriending the Vowbreaker, you, too, will meet your end—Chosen of Kali."

"Well, shit."

NINE

"Wait, I didn't commit any 'transgressions' against her people. What does this have to do with me?"

"I seem to recall you being there when we retrieved the runic neutralizer from Steigh Cea Styne."

"True, but I had nothing to do with your vow," I said. "Befriending is now a punishable offense?"

"They seem to operate by archaic laws of their own. Befriending a Vowbreaker in their eyes makes you just as guilty as the perceived Vowbreaker."

"I need to start keeping better company," I muttered. "The kind that doesn't get me killed."

"You could always join Bangers and Mash," Monty answered with half a smile. "I'm sure they would welcome your skill and expertise."

"I said the kind that *doesn't* get me killed, not the kind that races me to my death by C4—or worse."

"Just giving you options," Monty said. "Think of all the ways you can test your immortality with those two."

"Pass on joining the pseudo-mage and his sidekick. Not in that much of a rush to test my condition, thanks."

"I thoroughly expected this to be quashed, especially with the request I teach Cecelia," Monty said. "Apparently the Jotnar can hold a grudge."

"You think? Your apprentice has gone full Sith," I said, keeping my voice low. "How do we stop her? Without blasting her to bits."

"This Jotnar consciousness seems to have manifested because of Cecelia's shift. We just need to get her past the shift, and it should return to dormancy."

"That's all?" I said, shaking my head. "Doesn't sound complicated at all. What do we need to do?"

"First, we need to find Cecelia in this space."

"Right," I said, looking around. "You said she'd pick something familiar. This looks like a barren wasteland."

"I truly hope this isn't familiar to her," Monty said. "Even as empty as it appears, we need to be wary in here."

"Wary? Of what?" I asked. "This place is empty."

"Not exactly," Monty said, lowering his voice. "Do you recall the threat when we visited the Stynes?"

"You mean besides the unstable Jotnar trying to kill us?"

"Her cognitive degeneration and psychotic break were the results of her proximity to that ley-line. I meant the other threat."

"Honestly, it was all a blur. That usually happens when powerful ice women are trying to skewer me repeatedly with large ice missiles."

Monty grabbed my arm and pulled me to the side while gesturing with the other hand. A golden semi-circular wall of energy materialized in front of us as several angry-looking icicles slammed into it, shattering into dust.

"Move back," he said, covering his face as we backpedaled. "Do not breathe in that dust."

The pieces that fell to the floor weren't the familiar blue, glowing ice.

These shards were black.

That's when it came back.

"Shit, is that what I think it is?"

"Seems your memory has been jogged. Yes, *that* is obsidian ice."

"Obsidian ice, the fatal-to-magic-users kind of ice?" I asked. "Is that the signal to exit?"

"Would love to," Monty said, slowly panning his gaze. "Do tell me when you see the exit."

"It's right over...there." I turned to point to the entrance that was no longer there. "It was right over there. Come on, really?"

"See if you can contact your creature."

"I'm sure Peaches can hear me. Give me a sec."

<Boy, can you hear me? Are you close?>

I waited about thirty seconds before trying again.

<Hey, boy! Extra meat at the place if you can answer.>

"Anything?" Monty asked, gesturing.

"No response," I said. "He must be out of range."

"He's not the one out of range—we are."

"We are?" I asked. "Just how strong is Cece?"

"It's not Cecelia I'm worried about right now," Monty answered. "We need to break her focus."

"Okay, how do you—"

"Cecelia! Cecelia Styne! Desist from this course of

action this moment!" Monty yelled. "This is your teacher, and this behavior is inappropriate!"

"Spent much time around kids, have you?"

"She's not a child," Monty said. "The Jotnar consciousness inside of her is ancient, possibly millennia old."

"Inside the body of a child," I corrected. "Let me try. Just keep that wall up in case the angry, old Jotnar decides to unleash more black ice."

"Obsidian ice," Monty corrected. "Not black ice."

"Potato, potahto—bottom line, it's lethal."

"Granted," Monty said. "See if you can get her attention. I have an idea that may break the hold it has over her. I need to disrupt the focus."

Monty crouched down and began tracing symbols into the ground.

"Cece?" I called out. "Hello, Cece? It's me, Mr. Simon from next door."

I had a feeling "next door" was some distance from where we were standing at the moment.

"I just wanted to say thank you for helping Peaches find me when I was lost. Do you remember? How you, Rags, Peaches, and the tiny lizard, Frank, found me?"

It was petty, but I didn't care. Frank was no dragon, and I would remind him of that when we spoke, preferably after I smushed him a few times with my fist.

"Mr. Simon?" her small voice called out across the wasteland. "Is that you?"

I sensed her before I saw her.

"Over here," I said, waving an arm. "Hello, Cece."

She still looked around ten, thankfully. I didn't know what to expect when an ancient Jotnar consciousness took over a

Jotnar ice mage. Her white-blond hair flowed gently around her head. The air around her crackled with blue energy. It was Cece, but she was, like Peaches had sensed, more. Piercing sky—blue eyes looked at me with vague recognition.

She wore blue jeans and a black T-shirt with an image of Darth Vader holding a red light saber, framed by the Death Star in the background. I glanced down at Monty, who was still inscribing symbols.

"Vader, really?"

"Focus, Simon," Monty answered, keeping his voice low and his back to Cece. "I know that looks like Cecelia. It's also a powerful ancient Jotnar entity just waiting to unleash a barrage of obsidian ice at us. I'd rather avoid death by impalement today."

"Good point, Darth Monty."

"Mr. Simon?" Cece said. "Mr. Montague? What are you doing here?"

"Keep her talking," Monty said under his breath. "Just a little longer."

"It looks like you've been getting stronger," I said. "I don't really know where 'here' is. This is a place you've made."

"I made this place?" Cece asked, looking around. "Are you sure? This isn't home."

"I'm positive," I said, keeping my voice even. "Do you know how this happened?"

"No. I don't...I don't remember. I was practicing my homework with Rags..." A look of panic crossed her face. "Where's Rags?"

"Rags is safe," I said, watching the recognition leave her eyes. "She's with Peaches, who is watching over her."

"Rags would never leave my side, unless…Did you hurt her? Did you hurt my Rags?"

"Whatever it is you're going to do," I said under my breath, "you'd better do it fast, Monty."

"A few more seconds," Monty said, keeping his voice low. "Keep her talking."

"No, no," I said, raising my hands in surrender. "Rags is safe. She was trying to protect you when something happened. Can you try to remember what happened?"

Blue-white light erupted from Cece's eyes.

"I can tell you what happened, Chosen of Kali." Cece's voice had reverted to that of James Earl Jones. It kind of made surreal sense considering the shirt she was wearing. "Tristan Montague failed to honor his vow."

"Cece has left the building, Monty," I said as enormous, jagged shards of nasty-looking, obsidian ice slowly materialized, floating in the air surrounding us. "Monty?"

"Now—you die," Cece Earl Jones said.

I pressed the main bead on my mala bracelet and was treated to a significant lack of shielding.

"What the—?" I started as Monty slammed a hand into the ground.

Golden light blazed up from the symbols and raced across the floor to where Cece was standing. The light raced up her legs and enveloped her body, lifting her up into the air. Monty muttered some words under his breath and rotated his hand. The light shifted from golden to a deep violet, and Cecelia screamed.

The obsidian ice around us disappeared.

"You *will* honor your vow, Tristan Montague!" Cece Earl Jones roared. "I…have…time, mage!"

"Release her," Monty said, his voice full of menace. "She is not yours to manipulate. Let her go."

"She is Jotnar, and mine by lineage and right."

"She is my apprentice and under my tutelage," Monty answered. "Release her, before I destroy you."

"You cannot destroy me, mage. You are merely a child. I have existed for millennia. My power dwarfs—"

Monty rotated his hand again and the light turned from violet to black with red highlights. The energy around us shifted into nails-on-a-chalkboard territory, setting my teeth on edge. I saw drops of blood fall from Monty's nose. This was becoming bad.

"Monty?"

"Release...her," Monty answered, ignoring me. "Now."

"Very well, mage," bass voice Cece said. "I underestimated your resolve. I will not make the same mistake twice. The child will soon surpass even your power. When she does, she will be my instrument and your destruction."

"When she does, I will make sure she can send you to the outer depths where you belong," Monty said. "She will never be yours."

"Stronger mages have tried to resist the call and failed. Many have tried to banish me, yet still I remain."

"Enough. Release her."

Cece roared with her bass voice for a few seconds before her body hung limp. Monty rotated his hand back to the golden light setting, and she settled gently to the ground. She remained still for a few moments before stirring.

I saw Monty pull out a handkerchief and wipe the blood from his nose.

"Rags?" Cece asked as she opened her eyes. "Rags?"

Monty and I walked over to where she lay. She sat up slowly, rubbed her eyes, and stood.

"How are you feeling, Cecelia?" Monty asked softly. "Do you remember how you got here?"

"Yes," she said. "I was working on the runes you gave me to practice."

"Think very carefully," Monty said. "Did you change the runes or the order in which I gave them to you?"

Cece scrunched her face and nodded.

"Just a little bit," she admitted. "I found a shortcut."

"You found...a shortcut?" Monty asked, incredulous. "The rune sequence I gave you to work on was—"

"Too long, Mr. Montague," she said. "I changed some of the runes and removed others and still formed the circle. My way was faster."

"You changed...removed...runes from the sequence?"

I'd never seen Monty flustered. It would've been enjoyable if we weren't in an ice dimension, with some recently dispatched ancient angry entity floating around somewhere.

"I'm sorry, I thought the exercise was making the circle," Cece answered innocently. "You didn't say I had to do it exactly your way. Was I not supposed to change the sequence?"

Monty looked at her in silence for a few seconds.

"You were able to form the circle with your modifications?" Monty asked. "The same circle I showed you?"

"Well...mine was a little bit stronger than the one you showed me. Was that okay? It was still the same circle, yes."

"Stronger?" Monty asked. "I think we need to get back, now."

"What about the ice in The Moscow?" I asked. "And that circle that turned black—"

"The ice should be gone by now," Monty said, interrupting me and giving me a look. "We can discuss the rest after we get Cecelia back home."

"I'm all for that plan," I said, looking for the exit. "How exactly is that plan going to happen?"

"Cecelia is going to show me the modifications she made to the sequence I gave her," Monty said, looking down at the girl. "If she is correct, then we will go home."

"What if she's wrong?" I asked, suddenly not a fan of this plan. "What exactly is this sequence she modified?"

"If she's wrong," Monty began, "then we will end up lost in some pocket dimension—very much like this one."

I looked at Cece, who appeared unbothered by the fact that she had to create a circle to get us home or else lose us in some strange dimension.

"Cece, can you do this?" I asked. "I mean, really do this?"

"Yes," she replied, confidently. "I was doing that when the big voice messed with my circle. Up until then, my circle was correct, especially with my shortcut. My circle was better—no offense, Mr. Montague."

"None taken," Monty said with a slight nod. "I'm sure it was."

"Monty, I really don't think this is a good—" I started.

"Unless you know the way out or can contact your creature, it would seem that Cecelia"—he pointed at her —"is the exit from this dimension with her modified circle."

"Well, sh—sugar," I said, mindful of my audience. "I really hope you know what you're doing."

"I do," Cece said. "I think you should hold onto something, Mr. Simon."

She traced several runes in the air. The symbols materialized and trailed blue energy as they faded from sight. A large, blue circle appeared under our feet, the world tilted sideways, and the barren wasteland vanished from sight.

TEN

We arrived in The Moscow on our floor.

All of the ice was gone. The hallway was clear of debris, and everything was back to normal, with the exception of the missing door that led to Cece's place.

"We're back," I said, wincing with anticipation of the expected agony. "How did you do that with hardly any finger wiggles?"

"My shortcut," Cece said. "Can I see Rags now?"

"I'm sure she's outside waiting for you," Monty said. "Along with Simon's creature."

We headed downstairs and encountered a slightly less seething Olga in the lobby of the building, who turned at our arrival. Andrei stood at the door, giving Peaches a wide berth. I gave the lobby a quick once over, but didn't see Bangers and Mash on the property.

"Any sign of Bangersmash?" I asked, looking past the building entrance to see if the Pumpkin was parked outside. "Seems like they have left the area."

"I'm sure they had pressing business elsewhere," Monty said. "Plenty of buildings need blowing up."

"Is that like the mage credo?" I asked. "Maybe we should put that on our business cards? Strong and Montague—because plenty of buildings need blowing up."

"First of all, it's Montague and Strong, alphabetically. Second, that is not the mage credo."

"True. It's more like the mage way of life," I said, rubbing my chin and glancing at the glacial storm front approaching us in the form of an angry Olga. "We have ice incoming. Brace yourself."

Olga walked over to us and scowled at Cece.

"You almost break building," Olga said, looking first at Cece and then down at Monty. "Your student. You fix or move."

"I'm sorry, Aunt Olga," Cece said, eyes fixed on the floor. "I won't do that again in the building."

"Don't you think that's being a little harsh?" I asked. "She's only a little girl."

"Little girl?" Olga asked as the temperature in the lobby dropped by several degrees. "Building almost destroyed. This is little girl with big power."

"That's why she needs a teacher," I said, gesturing at Monty. "He is teaching her."

"Control, Stronk," Olga said, wonderfully mangling my name, her voice colder than the ice we had just faced. "Too dangerous if can't control. Many people in building in danger if it falls."

"She's right," Monty said, surprising me. "I'm going to need to put some extra safeguards in place if Cecelia is going to be exploring 'shortcuts' to the sequences I give her."

"Good," Olga said with a final nod. "You protect Cecelia and building—you stay. Can't protect? You go. Stronk go. *Persiki* monster dog go. Cecelia go back to family with chair-eating guardian."

Olga walked off and headed back to her office.

"What's a *persiki*?" I asked. "Why is she kicking me out if you can't control your Sith apprentice?"

"I think she was referring to your creature, and she's not a Sith any more than you are a Jedi."

"I'm totally a Jedi. Maybe even a Jedi Master. Do you think I should get a padawan, too?"

"And teach them what? The long-lost art of suicidal sarcasm?"

"*Persiki* means peaches," Cece volunteered. "She calls Mr. Simon *psikh,* but I don't think you look sick, if you ask me."

Rags and Peaches padded over to where we stood, and Cece ran over to greet her guardian.

"*Psikh* means nutcase or crazy, if I recall correctly," Monty said. "I know how you like to know these things."

"Really appreciate the translation—you could have kept that one to yourself, thanks."

"My pleasure. I know your stance on being ignorant of your names."

"How do you say 'psycho ice queen' in Olgese?" I asked. "Just in case."

"Just in case you've grown tired of breathing? I would strongly recommend against that course of action."

"Oh, she gets to call me nutcase and I can't return the favor?"

"She can probably freeze this entire structure faster

than you can get the words 'psycho ice queen' out of your mouth. Is that a favor you think you can deal with?"

"Fine, but I don't have to like it."

"Life is full of small compromises we make to maintain balance, and in your case, the ability to move freely without being frozen solid."

"Rags!" Cece said, raising her voice and hugging her guardian around the neck. "I'm so glad to see you're okay."

Being a Caucasian Mountain dog meant that Cece had to stretch to wrap her arms around Rags' neck. She managed, but just barely. Rags gently shook herself out of Cece's grip and stepped closer to me.

<Thank you for keeping the Miss safe. It appears the entity that attempted to control her has been dispatched.>

<You're welcome. Yes, Monty did the dispatching.>

<Without harming my charge—impressive. I owe you both a debt of gratitude. This does not include your hellhound.>

<He did remove you from harm's way.>

Peaches gave off a low rumble. Rags was not impressed.

<Was I in imminent danger?>

<I couldn't really tell. It looked like...>

<Then he did no such thing. What he did was remove me from the side of my charge when she needed me the most.>

<That's not exactly what happened. I told him to...>

<Thank you for keeping her safe. In the future, if there is another incident, please take the necessary steps to make sure I am conscious before trying to relocate me. Understood?>

<Yes. I still don't understand how I can hear you.>

<You are getting stronger. I'm sure the mage can explain it to you.>

<I'll ask him. I'm sure Monty has some questions for Cece as well. She found a shortcut to the sequence Monty gave her.>

<I told the Miss not to alter the sequence. Perhaps next time she will listen.>

<Unlikely, but good luck.>

I had the feeling that Peaches was going to have to be ultra-impressive to get Rags' admiration and attention. Something close to stopping a world-ending asteroid or facing a group of dragons—alone—might do the trick. Anything short of that would probably be dismissed by the super guardian.

"I'll escort them upstairs," Monty said, glancing at Cece. "I have a few questions about this 'shortcut,' and I need to install some stronger deterrents to runic manipulation by a certain Jotnar ice mage."

"I can show you my shortcut, Mr. Montague," Cece said, eagerly. "It really works!"

"Better let Olga know she needs to install a new door on Cece's place too."

"We need to discuss why shortcuts can be a dangerous thing," Monty said, leading her away to the stairs. "After I bolster the defenses in your home, and get you a new door."

"I'll get the Dark Goat," I called out before the door to the stairwell closed behind them. "Don't forget we have a meeting downtown."

Peaches nudged me, nearly launching me across the lobby.

<What?>

<I did rescue her.>

<Did you tell her that?>

<*I started with meat, but she only kept asking about the cold girl.*>

<*Did you tell her Cece was with Monty and me?*>

<*I tried, but she didn't listen.*>

<*So, you explained that you rescued her, didn't you?*>

<*I started with meat. She didn't care. How can she not care about meat?*>

<*She's a guardian. Cece is more important to her than any amount of meat. Just like I'm sure I'm more important to you than any meat—right?*>

<*What kind of meat?*>

<*Really? 'What kind of meat' is your answer?*>

<*You're my bondmate. You are important. Meat is important too.*>

<*I'm not even going to dignify that with an...*>

The energy signature that filled the lobby stopped me mid-sentence.

"It's rude to keep Death waiting, Simon."

I recognized the voice—Mori.

ELEVEN

"Hello, Peaches," Mori said, patting my hellhound on the head and managing not to have said arm removed. She reached into her bag and produced two large sausages. "Here you go."

Peaches gently removed them from Mori's outstretched hand and then proceeded to vacuum them into his bottomless pit of a stomach.

<Would you at least say thank you before stuffing your face?>

<Isn't it better to say thank you after stuffing my face? I won't know how the meat tastes until I eat it. What if it's like your healthy meat, and breaks my stomach? I don't want to say thank you if it's bad.>

It was hard to argue with hellhound logic.

<You say thank you before you stuff your face, to acknowledge the gesture. She thought about you enough to bring sausage.>

<That was very thoughtful. Should I lick her?>

<A small bark should be enough. Small—do not blast her across the lobby nor destroy the building. Olga would really kick us out if you did that today.>

Peaches hunched down and let out a small bark of thanks. The sound traveled across the lobby with a rumble, forcing Andrei to step outside in fear for his life.

<I said small.>

<That was small. I even made myself small.>

"Sorry about that," I said. "We're still working on communication."

"No need to apologize for him," Mori said, rubbing Peaches across the head and flank. "You and the mage, however, are making Ezra wait...not exactly the best idea. Did you not get my messages?"

"Messages?" I asked. "What messages?"

Mori was tall, and she was dressed in what I imagined was the combat version of Ezra's outfit. Under her jacket, dual shoulder holsters held two hand cannons and rested over a black Kevlar vest bristling with extra magazines.

Under the vest, she wore a dragonscale ensemble of black pants, a white dress shirt, and finished off with a pair of black Dr. Martens steel-toed Hynines. Mori stared at me as she pushed up the pair of glasses on the bridge of her nose. Her tight bun and icy glare reminded me of Karma. I shuddered involuntarily.

"Are you kidding me?" Mori said with a sigh. "Ezra sent you a message the moment you got back from your little trip overseas."

"We were headed to him when we were sidetracked."

"Sidetracked? It's like disasters follow the three of you. What happened?"

I explained about The Moscow and how it almost became The Rubble.

"Well, that's one way to miss my messages."

I nodded. "I couldn't even speak with Peaches," I said. "I didn't know she was that strong."

"This was the Jotnar child's doing?" Mori said, narrowing her eyes and examining the building. "Alone?"

"Monty says she hit a shift."

"No kidding, she hit a shift," Mori said, and let out a low whistle. "This complicates things. She almost took out the whole structure?"

"Complicates things?" I asked. "What do you mean, it complicates things? What does it complicate?"

"We will deal with that later. Right now—as in this moment—Ezra needs to speak to you and Tristan. Contact the mage."

I was reaching into my jacket for my phone when Monty walked into the lobby.

"Monty, this is—"

"Mori, Ezra's PA," he said with a short nod. "We've met."

"Of course you have."

"I take it your presence here means we've delayed longer than is acceptable?"

"Something like that," Mori answered. "Ezra would like...a word."

"Well, Simon, enough dallying," Monty said, looking at me. "It seems we don't have time to drive."

"You can't drive to where he is," Mori answered. "He's not waiting at the deli."

"Not at the deli?" I asked. "I thought he was *always* at the deli. Are you saying Ezra gets out?"

"Something you need to do more of," Mori said, shaking her head. "I understand why you delayed. It's just never a good idea to keep him waiting. Sort of a touchy issue with him. He prefers punctuality."

"Understood," Monty said. "Can you open a portal to him, then?"

I groaned, and then remembered that my last trip wasn't a gut-wrenching torture fest, threatening to remove my internal organs. Maybe I was getting the hang of this teleportation travel.

Mori slashed a hand in front of her and opened a portal. She stepped to one side and motioned for us to enter. Monty stepped in, followed by Peaches. I walked in behind them, and Mori followed me as the portal closed behind her.

TWELVE

We weren't standing in the deli. I looked around and found myself in a large garden, complete with trees, a running river, and a sizable lawn. A cool breeze could be felt winding through the trees.

I wasn't getting the hang of this teleportation travel. I took two steps before my intestines felt an overwhelming desire to exit my body. I grabbed my midsection and groaned as I found a tree to embrace.

"What's wrong with him?" Mori asked, glancing at me dispassionately. "Does he need a bathroom?"

"Teleportation sickness," Monty answered, waving a hand in my direction. "He's still in denial."

Peaches padded next to me and rumbled.

<Do you need some saliva? I have plenty.>

<I'll be fine, just give me a moment. Save the saliva for an emergency.>

<Your face looks like you are having an emergency. Are you sure?>

<I'm sure, thanks.>

Mori stepped close to where I stood doubled over and gently shoved the drooling Peaches to one side. She crouched down, bringing her face level with mine.

"You better get your shit together, Strong, and fast," she said, keeping her voice low. "What's coming your way won't give you time to 'catch your breath' or 'take a moment' to recover. You should be past this, Amateur Hour."

"Amateur Hour? Did you just call me—?"

"Thank you, Mori," I heard Ezra say as the pain subsided. "You may go."

"They're all yours," Mori said, opening another portal. "Have fun."

Mori disappeared a second later. Sitting on a long, wooden bench facing a small grove of trees, was Ezra, or as I knew him, Death...capital D.

"Simon, Tristan, thank you for coming on such short notice."

"Not like we had much of a choice," I said, glancing at him through the haze of pain. "We had a...situation. Well, Monty did at least."

Ezra wore his usual pair of half-moon glasses, and peered at me over the lenses for a few seconds, then shook his head. He waved a hand, forming a large titanium bowl filled with an obscene amount of pastrami—even for Peaches.

My hellhound fixated on the bowl and vibrated impressively in place instead of pouncing on the bowl. The warmth flushing my body didn't feel as effective as I recovered from my jump between planes. I chalked it up to consecutive trips. Maybe my body needed to recalibrate.

"There's some extra in there, because I'm sure he's been a good hellhound."

<I have been a good hellhound. Can I go eat it now? I am starving.>

<You've never starved a moment in your life.>

<Can I go eat now? I haven't eaten in hours. That's starving.>

<Mori just made you sausages. How are you starving?>

<That was a snack, not eating.>

<Only if you have a black hole for a stomach. I'm going to need you to do something for me.>

<What? Now? Don't you smell the meat? What do you want me to do?>

<Didn't you say it was best to make these requests under a dress?>

Peaches unleashed a small whine and added an extra dose of puppy-dog eyes.

<That's not fair. You don't think meat is life. What is it? You want me to eat more of the healthy meat?>

<Only if I want to put the greater tri-state area in danger. No. Here's the deal: you are going to get on an exercise program ASAP.>

<I get plenty of exercise.>

<Guess you really don't want that delicious bowl of scrumptious meat. Do you smell that? I'm sure it tastes incredible. I think I'm drooling a bit, just from the smell.>

<I agree. I will get on an exercise program.>

<On your word as my hellhound bondmate. Say it.>

<On my word as your hellhound bondmate, I will get on an exercise program.>

<You can thank Frank for that little lesson in whitemail.>

<You are devious.>

<Only when I need to be. I'd go eat if I were you, before Ezra decides to vanish the bowl with all that meat.>

Peaches pounced on the bowl and proceeded to inhale the meat with much smacking of the jowls. I turned to Ezra and gave him a nod of thanks.

"Like I was saying, we didn't really have a choice." I glanced over at Monty. "Someone's student was going full ice Sith on our building."

"She is not a Sith, ice or otherwise," Monty said. "But he is right—we had little choice but to attend to the matter immediately."

"There's always a choice," Ezra said, tapping the side of his nose. "It's living with the consequences of our actions that most people run from. Remember that."

"Duly noted," Monty said. "We made the choice to address the imminent destruction of our domicile before coming to visit you. My apologies."

"Apology accepted."

"Hey, that was actual diplomacy...and it worked."

"One day that mouth of yours is going to get you killed —several times," Ezra said, shaking his head. "You do realize silence is also part of diplomacy?"

"Discretion is the better part of valor?" I asked. "Similar to how I bravely traverse the planes with my slightly unstable mage partner and bottomless-stomached hellhound?"

"Not exactly," Ezra answered with a slight chuckle, "but you're getting there. If you don't accept what you are soon, the consequences will get more severe."

Ezra was dressed in his regular white shirt with black vest and black pants, his rune-covered yarmulke giving off a faint violet glow. Resting next to him on the bench sat a thick book.

It was easy to confuse him with an elderly scholar, and not the personification of Death—until he let you feel a minuscule amount of his massive, fear-inducing energy signature.

"Right now," I answered with a small groan, "the consequences of my actions are causing my digestive system serious agony."

"I'm sure, being acquainted with Karma, that you have an excellent working knowledge of cause and effect," Ezra said. "What you don't see yet, are potentialities."

"Excuse me?" I asked. "I'm not seeing what? Have you been speaking to Professor Ziller?"

"How was your trip abroad?" Ezra asked. "I understand Japan is exquisite this time of the year."

Ezra had a habit of doing that. I figured being Death meant his mind was occupied at all times. It was staggering he could even hold a conversation with us.

Every so often, in the course of our discussions, he would slip into what I assumed was a tangential topic, only to discover later on, that with Ezra, everything was connected.

"Japan was bloody and painful," I said, slightly thrown off by the question. "Thanks for asking."

"I hope not at the same time. I've noticed Ms. Nakatomi has not resumed her duties as Director of the Dark Council—yet."

"Maybe she's taking a well-deserved vacation?" I answered. "She did say she would be back. I didn't think pressing her for a start date was a good idea, considering the context."

"The power vacuum caused by her absence will need to be addressed if she does not return soon."

"Addressed?" I asked. "Why does *that* sound painful?"

"Only if you delay too long."

The feeling that struck me whenever Ezra mentioned that something needed to be "addressed" was similar to my reaction every time Monty wanted to have a "conversation" with an angry mage or felt the need to use "diplomacy" first—it felt like large doses of skepticism sprinkled with controlled dread.

It never ended well.

"That doesn't sound good," I said. "Can you go have some words with the current leadership of the Dark Council? Explain to them the error of their ways?"

"In what reality do you think my going to have words with any mortal will be welcomed as a good idea?" Ezra asked with a sigh. "Stop being a putz and pay attention. No one wants to 'have a word' with me, especially when it could be the last words they speak. You"—he pointed in my direction—"will eventually have to deal with this."

It never occurred to me that Death didn't really have anyone he could just chat with. It kind of made sense, though. no one was really eager to have a heart-to-heart with Death, and if he showed up to speak to you, well, it was likely the last conversation you were ever going to have. Puts a damper on the small talk thing.

"Me?" I asked, clearly confused. "Why would I ever dream of helping the Dark Council? They tried to take us out several times. Last time with a small army."

"Your vampire needs the Dark Council," Ezra answered. "More importantly, the Dark Council needs her, and the city needs a stable Dark Council."

"Still not seeing how this is my issue. I'm not a mage, vampire, or were-anything. How is this my business? Did I forget to mention that they threatened to kill Peaches and erase Monty?"

"Stop being so petty and look at the bigger picture here," Ezra answered, waving away my answer. "We both know those threats weren't credible. You've faced gods."

"We got lucky, multiple times."

"What do you think will happen if the Dark Council collapses?"

I imagined a city without the Council. The image wasn't pretty. They served an important and needed role in keeping the main factions of the city in check. As much as I wanted to see them blown apart, it would be in our best interests to have the Dark Council intact—for now.

"Nothing good," I said. "Still not seeing how this is my problem to fix."

"That's because you're dense," Ezra said. "In any case, that's a situation for another day. We have other issues to discuss."

"Other issues? Like what?"

It was always best to be transparent when speaking with Death. Things like "other issues" could easily be translated into "your imminent demise" if not made clear.

"Issues—like the golem."

THIRTEEN

"The what? Did you say golem?"

Monty cleared his throat. "That—is improbable," Monty said. "Golems are mostly the stuff of legend. They are impossibly complicated to construct and require more power than any one mage can command."

"You are mostly correct," Ezra said, looking at Monty. "If we were talking about the conventional method of creation."

"Maybe I misheard," I said, raising a finger and inter-rupting the conversation before it headed where I knew it was going. "Did you say Gollum, like *The Lord of the Rings*? My precioussss and all of that? Are you saying he's real?"

Monty gave me a *you can't be serious* look, which I returned with a *we just talked down a little Jotnar ice mage from a pocket dimension she created* stare. Mages—really.

"No, he's not," Ezra answered. "That's a character in a story. I'm talking about the other kind."

"The...other kind?" I asked, shaking my head. "I'm sorry, it's been an eventful day, what with preventing our building from becoming an ice sculpture, convincing a Jotnar ice child to rein in her super mage powers, and dealing with a pair of paranormal pretenders intent on blowing us all to Jersey or hell—same difference."

"That does sound eventful. How is little Cecelia?"

"Dangerous," I answered, "and powerful. Scary powerful."

"We'll have to revisit that at a later date," Ezra answered. "We need to discuss the golem."

"Sure, why don't I put that in my planner? Should I pencil that in after I fix the Dark Council, or before?"

"I'd put it in the 'things to do before I'm crushed' section, if I were you," said a voice behind me. "You were right, Ezra. He is exactly as you described him. I think he'll do nicely."

"Oh, great, now I sound like a pair of shoes," I said, turning to face a short woman who stared at me with eyes reminiscent of Syght. Her irises were milky white, but she didn't stumble around. "Speaking of shoes...where are yours? Wait a second—you're blind?"

She wore a simple brown robe with golden runes inscribed across its surface. I noticed hints of red, blue, and green runes appear in the fabric as she moved toward us.

Her bare feet seemed to float slightly above the ground as she walked. Her deep crimson hair was pulled back in a tight bun and held in place with what looked like small daggers—small, lethal-looking daggers.

"He's sharp, too," the woman said with a small smile and a bow. "Nothing escapes you, Simon."

"Like a butter knife," Ezra added. "This is Orahjene, highest elder of the—"

"Red Mountain Sect," Monty finished. "You're an elemental mage."

"Well met, Mage Montague of the Golden Circle," Orahjene said with another bow. "*Magus Bellum Ordaurum.*"

"I don't use that title any longer," Monty answered. "We are not at war."

"You are mistaken," Orahjene answered. "We are always at war."

"Okay," I said, holding up a hand. "That's our cue. Listen, Orajel, Orangina, or whatever your name is—"

"Orahjene, but you can call me Jen, if it's easier to remember."

"Sure, Jenny, now listen—"

"Jen or Orahjene," she interrupted, her voice hard. "No one calls me Jenny anymore."

"Sorry," I said, surprised at her reaction. "Jen."

"Simon," Monty hissed, "this is an elder of one of the most ancient sects in existence—"

"Tristan, please, let him finish," Jen said, raising a hand. "Please continue, Simon."

"Yes, *Tristan*, let me finish," I repeated. "It always starts this way. They hype you up with the, 'Help me, Obi-Wan Kenobi. You're my only hope,' line. Next thing you know some creature is trying to rip our faces off. Pass. Tell her, Monty—we pass. Whatever she's selling, we're not buying."

"I deeply apologize, Elder," Monty said with a bow. "Please forgive him. He's young and still ignorant of this world."

"Right, I'm the ignorant one," I said. "I'm going to remember my ignorance when something wants to rip your arms off and beat you silly with them."

Jen turned to Ezra with a nod.

"Yes, I agree with your choice, but I still need to see the core."

"Are you certain they can withstand your examination?" Ezra asked, giving me a concerned look. "He is still inexperienced."

"Examination? What examination? Who's getting examined?"

"They will face Toson," Jen answered. "I must be certain they can."

"Very well," Ezra said. "Who do you choose first?"

"Only him. The shieldbearer," Jen said, pointing at me. "He will make the choice. The mage is ready, but will falter without the immortal. So, it is set. Let it be done."

She turned and walked toward the lawn.

"Excuse me? What core? Who is Toson and what is she talking about? An examination? I've already had my annual physical."

"Be still," Ezra said, standing in front of me. "The Red Mountain sect is an elemental sect."

"I gathered that," I said, peeking around Ezra and looking at Jen, who had removed her robe to reveal what looked like a brown karate uniform underneath. "What is she doing?"

"She is going to task you with an urgent mission."

"What did I tell you?" I said, glancing at Monty. "Help me, Obi-Wan. Never fails. Can I just say no?"

"No," Monty and Ezra answered together. Ezra sighed and continued. "You haven't earned the mission yet."

"Is no one listening? I don't *want* this mission. I want to go home and sleep for about a week. Why doesn't she give this mission to Boobhead and Mulch or whatever their names are?"

"Your reluctance is precisely why she chose you," Ezra answered. "This mission...this adversary, will be dangerous. Not only physically, but mentally—he will attack you in ways you've never been attacked before."

"That's what she means about my core?" I asked soberly.

"Yes, that is what this examination is."

"By examination, does she mean like an in-depth interview? I can handle that."

"Not exactly," Ezra said, placing a hand on my shoulder. "The Red Mountain sect believes that the only way to know someone, truly know someone, is to engage in—"

"Excessive coffee drinking together?" I asked hopefully, knowing the real answer. "Let me guess, she doesn't really drink coffee, does she?"

"Not really, no."

"This is one of those fight to the death things, isn't it?"

Silence.

"Right," I said, cracking my neck. "At least that's not much of an issue. It's not like I stay dead."

More silence.

"This place is in stasis," Ezra explained. "Similar to what happens when you press your mark. Time stops, which means Kali's curse—"

"No longer applies. I'm mortal in here. Wonderful. Hey"—I looked around at the serene garden and river—"there are worse places to end it, I guess."

"The effects should be present by now."

"That explains why my digestive agony is still present. Or it could be the whole 'fight to the death' thing."

"I'm here for you, if that's any consolation," Ezra added.

"Are you serious? No offense, but that is the opposite of consolation," I said, shaking my head. "Are there any rules, or am I going to get blasted by elemental runes the moment we begin?"

"No magic, no firearms. Only bladed weapons."

Ezra waved a hand and produced a small, long case. He opened the lid and showed me the knives inside. They glistened with an internal light of their own. Both of the blades were identical. I had seen them before, in the hands of the Lucent who served Tartarus and tried to skewer me several times.

It was a pair of kamikira: god-killers.

FOURTEEN

"Thanks, but no thanks," I said, pushing the case away slowly. "I have my own blade."

"Which is a siphon, a seraph, and not allowed. I'm going to need you to place your blade"—Ezra removed one of the kamikira and waited—"in here."

I opened my hand and materialized Ebonsoul. Its black blade glistened as I placed it in the case and took the kamikira instead.

"Anything else?"

"Your other weapon, please."

I drew Grim Whisper and handed it to Ezra, holster first.

"I want to go on the record that I'm doing this under duress," I said, thinking back to my conversation with Peaches and smiling. "Also, this sucks."

"Understood," Ezra said with a small smile of his own, before growing serious. "Neither Tristan, Peaches, nor I can help you during this examination. Do you understand?"

"I'm on my own. Fighting to the death with a powerful elder, who needs to make me jump through hoops to make sure I'm worthy of handling a mission that will probably kill me, and those close to me—crystal clear."

"Good, you understand," Ezra said with a nod. "Tristan, any last words?"

"Really?" I said, staring at Ezra in disbelief. "Last words?"

"My apologies, that came out wrong," Ezra answered, stepping to one side. "I meant any final piece of advice you can share with Simon. Better?"

"Not really," I said, shaking my head. "I think we both need to get out more."

Monty stepped close.

"Red Mountain mages are adept martial artists, but most of them depend on their abilities and connection to the earth to supplement their techniques," Monty said, glancing in Jen's direction. "Use your observational skills, and break that connection. That is the only way you can get through this—alive."

Just what I needed before a fight to the death; convoluted magespeak advice on how to take down my opponent that made absolutely no sense.

"That was completely cryptic and demotivational, but thanks—I think."

"Remember: you are one with the force and the force is with you."

I stood there mouth agape. "You just Imwe'd me?"

"Remember our conversation about frequency?"

"Vaguely."

"This would be a good time to apply it."

"I would, if I even understood what you were talking about."

Peaches padded over and nudged my leg, gently, for the first time ever. That's when I knew this was serious. I crouched down and grabbed his massive head with both hands.

<I'll be okay, boy. She just wants to know if I'm flawsome enough to take this mission.>

<She wants to hurt you. If she hurts you, I'm going to bite her...hard.>

<No. You can't. Rules say you can't interfere. If you do, you'll get hurt. I don't want you to get hurt.>

<The rules are stupid.>

<I agree. Take care of Monty. Now, promise you won't try and bite her.>

<Only if I don't have to do an exercise program.>

<You are unbelievable, you know that? You can't go back on that, you promised.>

<You have to promise to come back—alive. On your word as bondmate.>

<On my word as bondmate. I promise.>

With Ezra by my side, I headed over to the lawn where Jen stood waiting. He extended the case and she took the other kamikira.

"When I step back, this area will be self-contained," Ezra said, waving a hand and forming an enormous circle beneath our feet. "The seal will only be broken when one of your energy signatures disappears, signaling death and the end of the examination."

"Understood," Jen said, moving to the other end of the circle. "I'm ready."

"Good luck, Simon," Ezra said, placing a hand on my

shoulder. "We've given you everything you need to pass this examination. Use that coconut you call a brain, and figure it out before she shish-kebabs you."

Ezra stepped out of the circle. A wall of sky-blue energy rose into place at the edge of the circle, enclosing Jen and me inside. I poked a finger at the wall.

It was as solid as steel when I pushed slow, but had some give when I jabbed a quick finger into its surface. It acted like some strange reverse non-Newtonian liquid. Unless I intended to run up and over the side of the wall in an extreme parkour move, I didn't see a use for it. There'd be no leaping through the energy at the edge of the circle.

"Ready?" I heard Ezra say, and Jen and I nodded. "Begin."

FIFTEEN

Several things didn't make sense in a hurry.

Why kill me if she wanted me for this mission? Why not just take Ezra at his word? It's not like his recommendation didn't carry a certain weight—he was Death, after all.

Something else was happening here and I was missing it. I took a deep breath and calmed myself. Jen stood across the circle observing me, which was creepy as hell.

I was used to the raving-lunatic-racing-at me kind of opponent, but she just stood there, absolutely still, and gazed at me. It was unnerving, because it made me realize I couldn't take her lightly. She was analyzing, extrapolating, and looking for weaknesses to capitalize on. It's what I would do.

If I attacked, I created more openings for her to exploit. If I stood still, I was working on her timetable. Damned if I did, and damned if I didn't. I took stock of the situation and slowed my breathing even more.

She was blind, but she could see. How? Is that why she was waiting? My movement would betray my location?

"Are you hoping I die of old age in here?" Jen asked. "Or maybe it's boredom?"

I declined to answer and remained still.

Goading tactics. Easily ignored. I focused on what her body was doing, not what she was saying. She stepped to the side staying close to the edge of the circle. I stepped to the side, maintaining equidistance.

She moved with a practiced grace only produced by years of training. I wasn't a slouch and had reached certain proficiencies with my prior training and, most recently, intensive training with Master Yat—although training with Master Yat felt like getting advanced lessons in pain tolerance.

I hefted the kamikira in my hand. The blade was perfectly balanced. The last time I faced one of these blades, my method of escape was leaping from a tall building in a single bound. I shook my head.

I really needed to re-evaluate my life choices. Deep down I knew Monty and Ezra were right. I needed to stop denying who and what I was, though that was easier said than done. I didn't ask to be cursed or thrust into the shadow world of mages, vampires, and gods.

Now, here I stood fighting for my life—again. It was becoming a habit I needed to shake. The problem was I didn't see a way out. I was in deep and getting deeper every day. Worse, people counted on me.

Even this examination was just another roundabout way of saying, "You're needed for this task". It wasn't the method I would've chosen, but I understood the motivation. This Toson character sounded like bad news. My question was, why couldn't Jen bring him down herself? I decided to ask and test a few theories.

"Why can't you take care of this Toson yourself?" I asked. "I'm guessing he's a Red Mountain mage like you."

"Toson is nothing like me," Jen answered without turning her head. "The only thing he wants and craves is power and death—specifically mine."

"Sounds like a great guy," I said, moving to the right a few steps. She moved the same distance to the left, which meant she was aware of my location without needing to hear my voice. "Maybe your sect needs to work on the recruiting process?"

"We are standing in an extension of my home," Jen said, taking a step forward. "I am currently undergoing a shift that will make me the First Elder of my sect. If I try to confront Toson in this state, not only will I die, but people close to me will perish as well."

"Mages and their shifts," I muttered under my breath. "Why not wait until after the shift, and then take him out?"

"By then, it will be too late," Jen said, shifting into a fighting position. "He will have summoned the golem and destroyed the Red Mountain, along with thousands of mages and their families. He planned this attack for this moment, knowing my vulnerability."

"If he's this powerful," I asked, "why isn't he becoming First Elder?"

"He's only so powerful because he stole an artifact— the Earth's Breath. As for being First Elder, why do you think he wants me dead?"

"Why me?" I asked, sliding into a matching fighting stance, but keeping my distance. "I have no dog in this fight, unless you piss off Peaches. Then you get more dog than you bargained for."

"I needed outliers," she said. "A blacklisted mage not interested in power, a reluctant immortal bonded to a hellhound. There could be no hint of impropriety. This is not a power grab. This is the rightful succession of Elders in my sect. You must not be connected to the Red Mountain in any way."

"I'd say we're about as improper as it gets."

"Exactly," Jen said. "I personally can't move against Toson, but you and Tristan can—if you pass this examination."

"And if I refuse?" I asked. This was the real test. "What happens if I walk away?"

"Several things: First, you need to defeat me in bladed combat to be able to leave this circle. This will be no small feat."

"You're that good?"

"Better," she answered without a hint of arrogance. "If you refuse to accept the mission after somehow achieving this, Toson will form the golem and destroy the Red Mountain sanctuary. Then, emboldened by this act, he will go to your city and attempt to kill you, and anyone important to you, for my seeking your assistance."

"This Toson really knows how to hold a grudge."

"You have no idea. With the Earth's Breath, he can form a golem army of indestructible, obedient soldiers that will follow his every whim. He will be unstoppable."

"What is it with mages and creating these overpowered artifacts?" I asked, exasperated. "Doesn't anyone stop to consider the ramifications of someone getting their hands on it and using it for evil?"

"Normals do the same thing. It's human nature."

"We don't create world-ending—never mind," I said, recalling virtually every invention we had transformed from scientific to military use. "Forget I said that."

"Forgotten," she said with a slight smile. "We are not so different from normals. I know our world is strange to you, but mages have fears and aspirations. We have dreams and families. We love and protect."

"And kill."

Her expression darkened for a few moments.

"Yes. We kill. When we lose our way or have to protect what is dear to us—just like you."

"There's also the small matter of you all being slightly unstable," I said, taking a step closer. She remained still. "Maybe no one is meant to manipulate that much power?"

"You will find agreement on that in both our worlds," Jen answered, turning slightly in my direction. "But there is no changing what is so for what we wish. We must deal with the present reality."

"This present reality...I'm guessing you want us to kill this Toson and get the Earth's Breath back?"

"Kill Toson? Not if it can be avoided. I only want you to get the Earth's Breath back."

"That's all?" I asked, surprised. "Just get it back to the Red Mountain?"

Jen nodded.

"That's everything."

She switched her grip on her blade and closed the distance.

SIXTEEN

Blade fighting is a messy, bloody business.

This situation was made worse by the fact that these blades were kamikira—god-killers. Getting cut by them was bad. Receiving a lethal blow meant death, of the permanent kind.

Despite the general consensus, I'd rather face a gun than a blade. In the hands of a master, blades were deadlier than any gun, and they never ran out of ammunition.

Jen was a master. The numerous cuts on my arms and legs spoke to her skill.

My mastery was in a different discipline—evasion. The numerous cuts on my arms and legs spoke to my lack of skill.

Holding her blade in a reverse grip, Jen slashed horizontally and then reversed direction. I avoided the initial slash and blocked the second, backhand attack with my own blade.

With our blades locked, she unleashed an uppercut with her free hand, its intention to remove my head from my shoulders. I slipped to the side, narrowly avoiding the rising fist, which suddenly switched into an elbow strike to the side of my head.

I ducked under the elbow and rolled back to give myself some breathing room. Unfortunately, that gave her breathing room, too, and she unleashed a side kick into my midsection, causing me to land on my back in a sprawl worthy of Peaches. I rolled to the side and back into fighting stance.

How was she seeing me?

"At this point you're wondering how I'm seeing you," she said, stalking me around the circle. "Yes?"

"The thought did cross my mind."

"It's actually quite easy," Jen answered. "Would you like me to share?"

"There are many things I'd like at this moment," I said, parrying a thrust, avoiding a feint, and rotating around another slash. "Doesn't mean I'll get them."

"It's...simple...really," she said with a grunt as we locked blades again. She stepped inside my guard, bent her knees, rotated her body, and flipped me over her hip and into the ground—hard. "I just close my eyes so that I can see better."

Stars danced across my vision. The body slam had forced the air out of my lungs as I crashed into the ground at her feet. I had no time to adjust, and rolled before Jen was plunging the knife downward, into the ground, where my chest had been a moment earlier.

"Just close your eyes to see better?" I asked, taking short gasps. "Answered just like a mage."

Jen laughed, then grew serious.

"If you don't figure it out, you're going to die here, Simon. I'm sorry."

"Not dead yet," I said, backing up. "Where are your shoes again?"

No answer—which, for me, was an excellent answer. Monty's words came back to me: *Use your observational skills, and break that connection. That is the only way you get through this—alive.*

"You never mentioned what kind of mage you were," I said, working out the trajectory of using the walls for my next attack and feint. "See, little Cece is an ice mage. Makes sense, considering she's a Jotnar. Monty, I've seen use fire, water, and air."

I wasn't going to mention the blood magic. I figured that would make Monty look bad, and he didn't need any more negative press.

"You forgot the blood magic," Jen said, sliding in. "I expected no less from a shieldbearer."

"Dammit," I said under my breath. "How did you know?"

"It taints him," Jen said. "Like you, he will have to confront that aspect of who he is eventually. It is inevitable."

"He's not a dark mage."

"I never said he was."

"This whole thing with Toson, the Earth's Breath, and your being from the Red Mountain only leads in one direction for an elemental mage. You use the earth in some way."

"Well done," Jen said. "That was much sooner than I expected. Not that it will save you."

"This whole circle is a Kobayashi Maru, isn't it? There's no way for me to win."

"You have to die, yes," Jen answered, coming at me. "I'm glad you've made peace with your demise."

"Well, shit."

I turned and ran at the wall. She was a few feet behind me and closing. I managed three steps up the wall and pushed off, reversing direction. The moment I was airborne she froze, searching for me.

I buried my blade in her side before I landed next to her. Her reaction was immediate. She grabbed my wrist, crushing it, and trapped me next to her. She slid, planting a foot behind her and rotated her entire body into the perfect hammer throw—with me playing the part of the hammer. I flew across the circle at what felt like terminal velocity and crashed into the far wall. It was time for the feint.

I lay perfectly still and focused on my breathing. This was one of the early exercises Master Yat had beat into me. Control the breath. Control the fight.

His words rushed back even as I made myself one with the ground, the energy of the circle, the vibrations in the air. I emptied my mind and became no thing and everything: *Simon, mushin no shin—the mind without mind—is the state you must achieve when you fight. You must be constantly flowing without stopping anywhere. The moment you stop this flow...you will meet Death.*

It was the hardest paradox for me to understand... until now. By stilling myself, it allowed me to connect to the flow of everything around me. For a few brief moments, I altered my frequency and camouflaged my energy signature to such a degree that I disappeared—it also helped that I was near unconsciousness from being flung into the wall. I had, for all intents and purposes, died.

Jen approached, crouching down next to me. She lay her kamikira near my head, placed a hand on her wound to stop the bleeding, and the other on my chest. I felt the energy at the edge of the circle drop. To her credit, her reaction time was phenomenally fast—just not fast enough.

I reached up and hooked a hand behind her neck while flinging a leg around her waist, causing her to pitch forward. She outstretched an arm, stopping herself, reached to the side for her blade, but was too late. I held it to her neck.

"Well done," Jen said as Ezra, Monty, and Peaches approached the circle. "You have passed the examination."

I let her go, fell back, and laid in the grass, admiring the cloudless azure sky.

"That sucked. No offense."

"What have you discovered about yourself today?"

I sat up slowly. The warm flush of healing I was accustomed to was missing, replaced with a dull ache all over my body.

"After much self-evaluation, I've realized that deep down, I really, truly, dislike examinations."

She chuckled and then grew semi-serious.

"Well said," she answered. "I, too, dislike them."

"Really? That's not what was coming across as you were pounding me all over the circle. It seemed like you were enjoying yourself."

"Well, a little," she confessed with a nod. "It's been a while since I've been able to fight with someone. No one would dare enter a battle circle with an Elder. It's just not done."

"You really ought to hook up with Master Yat," I said. "He has no problem beating on people."

"Master Noh Fan Yat is an old friend."

"I'm not surprised," I said with a groan. "You share similar beating philosophies."

"He and his infernal stick *are* memorable."

It was my turn to chuckle, which I regretted instantly.

"Why?" I asked. "What was the purpose of all this?"

Her face darkened.

"Toson will try to kill you," she answered, looking over at the approaching trio. "If he can't, he will attack those closest to you and any he deems an obstacle."

"I'm familiar with the method, trust me."

"You can't reason with him or appeal to his sense of justice or fair play. There is only one truth—his truth."

"You couldn't just tell me that?" I asked. "Even an email would've been good...really."

"No, I couldn't. You needed to know this was possible. You needed to experience"—she waved an arm at the circle around us—"a circle of death."

"Can we not do that again...ever?"

"The skills you tapped into while facing me, are the skills you will need to face Toson and his golem."

"Fear and an extreme sense of self-preservation?"

"Observation, deduction and extrapolation," she said, getting shakily to her feet. "He has few weaknesses and the golem fewer still. How did you figure it out?"

I stood slowly, careful not to aggravate my assortment of injuries. I really needed a large cup of coffee and a nap.

"Bare feet allow you to have a connection to the earth,"

I said. "Your melee style of fighting means you like to be close to your opponent, feel where they are. Nice throws, by the way."

"Thank you," she answered. "That was a calculated risk. What if you were wrong?"

"Like Ezra said, the best way to know someone is to fight them."

"You managed to cut me," Jen said, touching her side gingerly. "But you weren't fighting to kill."

"Neither were you," I said. "Trust me, I can tell the difference."

"I'm sure you can. Toson will not afford you such mercy. How did you know to attack from the air?"

"I figured, being an Elder your skill was high enough that you could probably sense air vibrations too, but relied mostly on your connections to the ground."

"Impressive," she said. "That explains the aerial attack."

I nodded. "For a few seconds, I hoped you'd lose me while I was airborne. Even if you could detect air vibrations, it was my only window of attack."

"When you face Toson, there will be no rules. He will use all of his abilities to destroy you. You cannot hold back."

"I don't intend to."

Peaches bounded over to where I stood.

<You're alive. That's good. I thought she was going to hurt you.>

<She kind of bounced me on the ground a few times, but I'm mostly okay.>

<If you ate more meat, you could be bounced and not get hurt. Do you want me to lick you?>

<I'm going to pass on the drool therapy for now. I just need to leave this place and my body will start to heal.>

<Can we go to the place? I'm hungry.>

<You just ate.>

<My hunger is in the present. The meat I ate was a long time ago.>

<Long time ago? Are you kidding?>

<You need to eat more meat in the present. Then you wouldn't get hurt because the meat would make you strong.>

<Your Meat Zen is way past my ability to understand.>

<You need to make your understanding elevators. That is the beginning.>

"There have been developments," Ezra said. "The violent kind."

"Developments?" I asked. "What developments?"

"The golem has been spotted in the city," Ezra answered, his voice grim. "It would seem Toson has altered his plans."

"He's removing anyone that could help me defeat him," Jen said. "It's too late. Secure your city and get to safety. The golem is unstoppable."

"No one attacks my city," I said. "No one."

"You don't understand—the golem can't be stopped," Jen said. "Ezra, send me back I will begin the fortifications."

"I can't," Ezra said. "Not until your shift is done. The risk is too great, to you and to the Red Mountain. You are no use to your people dead."

"There must be a way to stop this creature," Monty said. "Nothing is unstoppable."

"There is one way," Jen said, "but it's too dangerous. You would be throwing your lives away. The plan was to stop Toson *before* he created a golem. Everything has changed now."

"In what way?" Monty asked. "Tell me."

"If Toson has created a golem, it means that the Earth's Breath is in play," Ezra said. "He's using it to control the golem."

"It's an ancient artifact," Jen answered. "In order to use it, the artifact siphons life-force from a victim, draining them until death."

"How is he powering this artifact?"

"If the golem is present, he is using the artifact to make himself powerful," Jen answered slowly. "The only way to do this is to siphon other mages."

"Mages?" I asked in disbelief. "This thing made him the equivalent of a mage vampire?"

"That's an oversimplification, but yes," Jen said. "You understand now why you can't confront him? Especially you, Tristan. Toson will be wearing the artifact. You have to remove it from his body. The moment you attempt this, the golem will move to protect him—by killing you."

"I'm going to have to agree with Simon on this...no attack on this city will go unanswered," Monty said. "Ezra? If you could facilitate a portal, please."

"Of course," Ezra said, waving a hand and forming a portal that led back to The Moscow. "Are you certain about this?"

"No," I said. "Facing a golem wasn't the mission, but it seems like we have limited choices now."

"You're beginning to understand," Ezra said, nodding and handing me Ebonsoul and Grim Whisper. "Remember what you learned here. It will be useful when you face Toson."

"I'll try. It's not like I can remember every——"

Ezra whacked me upside the head with a gentle tap.

"Do or do not——there is no try."

With another wave of his hand, the portal wrapped itself around us, disappearing the garden.

SEVENTEEN

We arrived inside our office.

I waited a few beats for the agony to commence and... nothing. Peaches roamed off to our reception sofa and performed a magnificent sprawl, taking up half the sofa. Several seconds later, he started snoring.

"Did Ezra just Yoda me?" I asked when I felt the rush of warmth flood my body, healing my recent injuries. "He totally Yoda'd me."

"I have no idea what you're referring to," Monty said, pulling out some books from our library. "We need to research this Earth's Breath artifact. I have to contact the Professor."

"Ziller?"

"Is there another Professor we know that could have information on an ancient artifact belonging to the Red Mountain?"

"Good point," I said. "Hey, my body isn't in agony. Maybe you can take some portal classes with Ezra?"

"Or maybe you're just finally accepting you aren't a normal any longer."

The words hung in the air for a few seconds.

"It's because Kali cursed me," I answered after a pause. "This was beyond my control."

"Irrelevant," Monty answered without looking up from a book. "The cause doesn't change the outcome. The curse has made you different. You aren't normal. I suspect you were abnormal even before Kali touched you."

"Oh, ha ha," I answered. "There's that cutting British humor. The hilarity is killing me—figuratively."

"Why don't you make yourself useful and see if there have been any reports or sightings of this golem," Monty said, ignoring my comment. "Maybe call the NYTF or the Dark Council? Hmm?"

The New York Task Force, or NYTF, was a quasi-military police force, created to deal with any supernatural event occurring in New York City.

If anyone had any idea about the golem, it would be them or the Dark Council. But without Chi currently leading the Dark Council I was reluctant to reach out to them on account of they actively had plans to kill me and Peaches, and Monty.

On our visit to Japan, Chi had told me it was mostly a bluff. The small army that had descended on our location downtown said otherwise. Someone in the Dark Council wanted to retire the Montague and Strong Detective Agency—permanently.

The NYTF were paid to deal with the things that couldn't be explained to the general public without causing mass hysteria. They were led by Angel Ramirez, who was one of the best directors the NYTF had ever had, and still, surprisingly, my friend. We had a history. Most of it good, some of it bad, and a small amount classified. It was keeping Angel in the dark about that last part that kept him safe—and alive.

Since our skirmish downtown with the Dark Council Enforcers, and then an emergency trip to Japan, Angel and I hadn't spoken. I didn't look forward to the call. He was usually pissed—with good reason. Although this time, we had nothing to do with this golem.

"Good idea," I said. "Right after a cup of Deathwish to fuel my brain."

"For once, you've made a sensible suggestion."

"You're going to drink coffee?" I asked, surprised. "You've finally come to your senses. Took you long enough."

Monty looked up, and glared.

"Don't be daft," he snapped. "Kindly put the kettle on to boil. I could use a strong cuppa."

I headed to the kitchen when my phone rang.

"Speaking of the NYTF," I said, looking down at the number and wincing. "Ramirez."

"Perfect," Monty said, his face buried in a book again. "See what he wants. Maybe he has a location for this creature. That would save us time."

I connected the call.

"Angel," I said, keeping my voice light. "How are you?"

"How am I? How am I?" Angel answered, his voice escalating with every syllable. "I'll tell you how I am!"

I put the phone on speaker to prevent him from blowing out my eardrum.

"Take a breath, Director."

"Don't 'take a breath' me, Strong. Do not...tell me...to take a breath."

"Fine, stop breathing. Don't blame me when you pass out."

"Just out of curiosity," Angel asked, "when did you two get back?"

"What makes you think we were away?"

"The peace and quiet that descends on my city whenever you, your mage, and that oversized canine you call a pet are away, makes me think that has been the case."

"Whatever it is," I started, "we don't have anything—"

"Somehow you're connected. Don't try to bullshit me, Strong. I have reports of a large stone creature destroying everything in its path...in my city."

"Like I said, we don't have—"

"And then just out of pure coincidence I call to see if your detective agency is in the city, and what do you know? You're open for business! Imagine the odds."

"Did you say a large stone creature?" I asked, ignoring the mostly baselessly accusatory tone of his voice. "Are the attacks arbitrary?"

"Actually, no," Angel said, after releasing a long sigh. "That's just the general press release. So far it's only attacking at night; we're mixing that with gas leaks and faulty wiring where we can, and deflecting everywhere else."

"That won't last very long."

"Word on the magical street is that your mage summoned this thing."

"What do you think?" I asked, letting my voice get hard. "Is that what you think?"

"I think it's dangerous to my city and the people in it.

Your mage has done some crazy shit in the past, but nothing this crazy."

"Monty didn't summon it."

"Does he know who did?"

"We have some leads we are following. I'll definitely keep you in the loop."

Ramirez groaned on the other end, and I could picture him rubbing his hand down his face.

"You do that, Strong," Ramirez said. "*Before* the city is on the verge of destruction, not after you've blown half of it to bits."

"Will do," I said, having no intention of getting Ramirez or the NYTF involved in facing a golem. "Can you get me a list of the areas attacked or destroyed?"

"Sure," he said, hitting some keys on his computer. "Maybe you'll have better luck than we did. My analysts can't make heads or tails out of the locations being targeted."

"Thanks, I appreciate it."

"Oh, one more thing," Ramirez said, and I braced myself for another ranting scream fest. "Maybe you can shed some light on a pair of new players in the city"—I heard the clicking of keys again—"Boogers and Mush... That can't be right. They claim to be paranormal investigators, or something like that."

"Bangers and Mash, and they're mostly harmless, except for the insane amount of C4 they carry around."

"What the hell kind of name is Bangers and Mash— wait seriously? Did you say C4?"

"Yes. They drive around in an orange VW Bus, and I'm guessing it's loaded with ordnance," I said. "One or both must be sensitive and have some minor ability."

"Did you happen to get a license plate?"

"It's BNGRMSH. I kid you not."

"Right," Ramirez answered. "I'll have my people pick them up, confiscate the explosives and run the paranormal investigator license interview on them. That should scare them out of the city."

"That's cruel and devious," I said, suppressing a laugh. "Have fun."

"Strong, stop this moving mountain from breaking my city. My men are powerless against it. If you can't do anything, I'm going to have to speak to Ken over at the Dark Council."

"I understand, Angel. You do what you feel is necessary, but don't trust them."

"I don't. I barely trust you, but you get results."

"Thanks. I'll give you a call as soon as I know anything."

EIGHTEEN

"I can't believe he threatened me with going to the Dark Council," I said after ending the call. "They don't care about this city."

"I'm sure they could say the same thing about him working with us, considering your destructive track record."

"*My* destructive track record? What?"

"What exactly is a paranormal investigative license interview?" Monty asked. "I don't recall Ramirez ever requiring us to go through this process."

"It's basically a non-existent interview process where Ramirez vets rookie sensitives who take it upon themselves to go out and 'save the city' from all threats."

"I take it not many pass this interview?"

"None, so far," I said with a grin. "But, I'm sure Angel has saved dozens of lives with it. Most of these rookies know just enough to get themselves killed."

"I'm going to contact Professor Ziller," Monty said,

still holding the book. "I'd be interested in seeing that list of destroyed properties."

"You think it's connected?"

"I do," Monty said. "I'm certain the Professor will have more insight, though."

He stepped over to the closet near the door, looked inside, and closed the door again with a satisfied nod.

"You're checking to make sure the closet door works properly?" I asked. "We do have maintenance people for that sort of thing. Unless you're taking up home improvement now."

"The seal needs to be precise. This door is adequate."

"I recall Jen was bouncing me around in the secret garden; I just don't recall you suffering a head injury lately. What are you talking about?"

"I need a properly closing door in order to call the Professor."

Monty traced golden symbols on the closet door, which glowed brightly and faded after a few seconds.

"Well, that was pretty," I said. "Maybe we can rent you out for kids' birthday parties?"

Monty lifted a finger and glared at me.

"Patience. Professor Ziller will be here shortly."

The edges of the closet door blazed with golden light as the door shuddered in place. I took a few steps back as the shuddering increased and then suddenly stopped. The door opened, and a figure emerged from the closet.

He was dressed pretty much the same way I remembered when I last saw him. He wore librarian casual—jeans, a long-sleeve white shirt and construction boots. His sandy-brown hair was a little thinner on top, and he sported a goatee and what appeared to be a rune-covered monocle—which was new.

He held a nearly transparent orb in his hand as he squinted at us. Light blue arcs traveled around his body in random patterns. They reminded me of TK and her black and green energy; only, these arcs felt more in the "keep away or I'll blast you" department, unlike TK's, which resided squarely in the "breathe in a way that displeases me, and I'll reduce you to a memory" category of energy.

He tossed the orb up and it floated next to his head, following as he moved forward into our reception area, carrying with him the smell of old books. Behind him, in what used to be our closet, I could see rows and rows of books and hear the sounds of rustling paper.

"That's like the Moving Market," I said, looking in awe at the Living Library's book repository, now occupying our closet. "Hello, Professor Z."

"It is a pleasure to see you both again," Ziller said, looking at us and sitting on the large reception sofa partially occupied by a snoring hellhound. This reception sofa sat opposite what I liked to call Roxanne's sofa—the Hansen.

The Hansen sofa had been a gift from Roxanne to Monty, and it was the most expensive item in our reception area. No one was allowed to sit on it, except Roxanne on her infrequent visits. Even Peaches respected the boundary set by Roxanne. He was a smart hellhound.

"Welcome, Professor Ziller," Monty said. "It's good to see you."

"Thank you," Ziller answered with a slight cough. "Could I trouble you for a spot of tea? I'm terribly parched."

"Of course," Monty said, heading to the kitchen. "I'm sure we have some digestive biscuits laying about."

"That would be exceptional," Ziller said. "Thank you."

Monty headed into the kitchen while I busied myself with the inner workings of the closet, now library.

"Professor, I'm not seeing the biscuits," Monty called from the kitchen and glancing my way. "How much time do you have? I'm sure we can get some. I could have sworn we still had some—Simon?"

Yes, I ate the digestive things he called biscuits. To me, they looked liked big cookies. The taste could have been better, but they were great with coffee. Like every person living with a large animal, and looking to dodge blame, I confessed Peaches' crime for him.

"Peaches must have gotten into them," I said, paying extra attention to the enormous library currently occupying the space of our closet. "I'll have a word with him when he wakes up."

"Really?" Monty said. "I'm surprised he could ingest anything other than meat. It must have been quite difficult for him to reach the top shelf of the cupboard, what with having no opposable thumbs and all."

"Hellhounds...crazy resourceful," I said with a shrug. "What can I say?"

"I understand you may be pressed for time, Professor. Will the tea suffice?"

"The tea is fine, thank you. Time is such a fluid concept, Tristan," Ziller answered after a pause. "The digestives can wait for another visit—but did you inquire about time?"

That pause—which I figured was the moment Professor Z took to process all the permutations of where he was in the time-space continuum, in relation to all the other Zillers on all the other parallel realities—was the start of my brain-melting headache.

"Here we go," I muttered under my breath. "Once he gets going..."

"Are you referring to the indefinite, continued progress of events that occur in what is apparently an irreversible succession from the past, through the present, and to the future?"

"Do you see what you started?" I asked, glaring at Monty. "You know where this is headed."

"Or were you referring to time on the quantum level, where it is posited that past, present, and future occur simultaneously?"

Monty gave Ziller a quick glance before answering.

"Yes," Monty said, pouring hot water and doing what I thought impossible. He made Professor Ziller pause long enough in his train of thought, to create an opening. Monty swept in deftly, like a master of Quantum Ziller wordfu, and asked a question. "What do you know about the Earth's Breath?"

"The Red Mountain sect artifact?" Ziller answered, getting completely sidetracked. "The war weapon?"

"The same," Monty answered, bringing over a cup of tea. "Properties, abilities, and weaknesses."

"Tristan, that is a dangerous artifact. One you do not want to manipulate."

"We may not have a choice," I said. "It's been stolen from the Red Mountain."

"Stolen?" Ziller said, before taking a sip of tea. "I hadn't heard of this, but it may be possible I'm on a different timeline. Moving the Library gets complex at times."

"I can only imagine," I said, not understanding it all. "I have no idea how you keep it all straight."

"Practice, mostly."

"Professor, we're under a bit of time pressure ourselves," Monty said. "The Earth's Breath?"

"Right, right," Ziller said, placing the cup down on the table and reaching for his orb. "I should have it right here...one second. You do understand that time is an illusory construct?"

"I remember the lessons," Monty said. "Time is an artificial construct and as such only exists in very limited contexts."

"You always were a good student—ah, here it goes."

Ziller pressed the surface of the orb and an image of a turquoise cube gently rotated above the table. The polished cube hung from a golden chain. Each surface of the cube was inscribed with a golden rune I couldn't understand.

"Is that it?" I asked, looking at the simple cube. "It looks so...unassuming."

Ziller lifted the monocle to his eye as the runes on it's surface glowed softly. He peered at the image closely and nodded.

"That's the Earth's Breath in its dormant state," Ziller said, pointing. "One of several artifacts classified as vampiric essences."

"Vampiric essences?"

"The Earth's Breath, like all artifacts of this classification, requires life-force to execute its functions. In the case of this artifact, the vampiric quality is transferred to the object of its creation—the golem."

"Which are?" Monty asked. "What are the main functions?"

"This is a war weapon, created at the height of the Supernatural War. Its main function is to create an army of indestructible soldiers—golems. These golems can be controlled by one mage, specifically an elemental mage."

"Weaknesses?" I asked. "How do you stop it?"

"Several ways," Ziller answered. "Kill the mage wielding it, very difficult; deny the artifact the life-force it needs to function, also near impossible since it's always in a state of siphoning once activated; or destroy the golem or golems created by it. The last act will send the artifact into a state of short dormancy."

"How long?" Monty asked. "How long will the artifact be dormant?"

"Three to five days, depending on how many golems were created. The more golems created, the longer the dormancy period. It is never shorter than three days, however."

"What happens after three days?" I asked. "Does it reboot?"

"Something similar," Ziller answered, before standing and making his way back to the closet. "If there is a power source nearby, the artifact can be reactivated. Without a golem it will draw energy from the nearest source—a mage."

"Wonderful," I said. "Anything else we should know?"

"A few. An artifact this powerful needs an enormous amount of energy to activate. This city with its hubs would be ideal for that."

"Hubs?" I asked. "What hubs?"

"Several of the nexus points in this city act as hubs, amazing reservoirs of power. If an elemental mage attained the Earth's Breath and wanted to use it alone, these hubs would be ideal without sacrificing their own life-force."

"The attacks," I said, remembering Ramirez's words. "The golem is attacking hubs. That's why Toson came here first."

"If I were this mage, I would have come here first," Ziller agreed. "The hubs in this city are incredibly powerful. It must be the concentration of energy. I'll have to write a paper on that one day."

"Professor," Monty said, getting his attention again. "Anything else?"

"This is a war weapon. If he has created a golem he will have to be close to it," Ziller said. "This is not a fire-and-forget weapon. The risk of out-of-control golems was too great. Limiters were introduced into its creation."

"Such as?" Monty asked. "What are the constraints?"

"Proximity and line-of-sight control. The wielder must be no more than three hundred yards away and maintain sight with the golem."

"And the siphon?" Monty asked. "Where does it originate?"

"The siphoning aspect switches from the artifact to the golem once the golem is created, making it impossible for a mage to approach an active golem."

"What happens if those conditions are altered?" I asked. "Three hundred yards is still far."

"If either of those conditions are changed," Ziller continued, "the golem ceases to function. It becomes, in effect, a very large, if potentially lethal, sculpture."

"Does it have any ranged attacks?" I asked. "I'm not looking to get barbecued by this thing with some flame breath."

"Golems aren't dragons, Simon," Monty answered. "I'm certain we—"

"Don't get close to it if you're a mage," Ziller said, glancing at Monty. "It actively seeks out mage life-force. Oh, and one more thing, the mage wearing the Earth's Breath has heightened control of his chosen elemental discipline—usually earth."

"How powerful do they become?" I asked, dreading the answer. "Are we talking Super Saiyan God here?"

"I'm not entirely familiar with the term Super Saiyan,"—Ziller glanced the question at Monty, who shook his head with a sigh—"but this Toson should be about a shift or two away from an Archmage," he continued, returning the cup to a table and opening the door to the closet. "If at all possible, engage from range and use stealth tactics. If you can remove the mage's eyes—you might stand a chance."

"Thank you for your assistance," Monty said. "It's been quite...illuminating."

"My pleasure," Ziller answered. "Thank you for the tea."

He stepped into the closet, closing the door behind him. The edges blazed with light again, followed by less shuddering. When I opened the door, it was our closet again.

"Did he really just say 'remove his eyes' and we can stand a chance?" I asked, closing the closet door. "The Professor is a little dark these days. Don't you think?"

"He's always been that way," Monty answered. "Super Saiyan God? Really?"

"Just trying to wrap my non-mage melted brain around this situation."

"By using obscure manga references?"

"Goku is not obscure," I said, defensively. "If he were here, he would fight the golem, get his ass kicked, go into training, come back stronger, and then kick the golem's ass. This would be followed by more training so he could face the 'one shift away from an Archmage' Toson."

"Maybe this Goku can join Bangers and Mash, and together they can stop this threat from destroying our city?" Monty asked. "Perhaps together they can form a new Ginsu Force?"

"You do know Goku is a fictional character, right? And it's Ginyu, not Ginsu. This isn't a group of kitchen knives, it's a—"

I stopped at his expression.

"Please, do go on," Monty said, after sipping more tea. "You were expounding on the complexities of fictional manga characters and their relationship to... cutlery?"

"Maybe I do need to get out more."

"You are incorrigible," Monty said, nodding. "At least the Professor shed some light on the attacks on the city. Toson is fueling his army."

"What's the plan?" I asked, opening and closing the closet door a few more times just to make sure Ziller was really gone. "Toson is a hard target."

"We need to stop a golem army from forming."

NINETEEN

"Can we really take on a golem?" I asked. "I mean, I know you're strong, but are you golem-stomping strong?"

"Toson's too strong, and I suspect the Earth's Breath is feeding off of him even as it supplies him with power," Monty said. "The only course of action is to stop the golem and send the artifact into dormancy. Then, we can confront Toson. Did you get the list of destroyed properties?"

I checked my computer and pulled up the email Angel sent. It was a list with a corresponding map of the locations targeted by the golem. I handed the printed version to Monty, who began examining the document.

"How about we help accelerate Jen's shift," I started. "Then, she can go out and crush Toson all on her own? Case closed."

"There are no shortcuts to a shift...wait a minute," Monty said, looking up from the paper he held. "You may have given us another option."

"I know," I said. "Jen, shift, and crush. We avoid angry,

dangerous stone man and psycho mage. Then, we go some-where warm for vacay? I'm sure Roxanne would love to get away."

"There will be no 'vacay'," Monty said, waving my words away. "As for speeding up the Elder's shift, that's preposterous. We can't accelerate a shift."

"How about nudging it just a bit?"

"Even attempting to do so can have catastrophic results. Imagine Cecelia's powers out of control, only to the power of ten."

"Okay, I'm going to go with no on the shift accelera-tion for two hundred, Alex."

"However...The runes on the Earth's Breath, I recog-nized them. There may be a way to short circuit the arti-fact into dormancy, but it will be risky."

"Oh, that's a surprise," I said, completely not surprised. "That sounds great, if I understood what it was you were talking about. What do we need to do?"

"We need to go see a certain Jotnar ice mage child with a penchant for runic shortcuts."

"Hopefully we can do this without the deep freeze?" I asked. "I've really had enough ice to last me several lifetimes."

"After that," he said, looking down at the paper again, before putting it in an inner pocket, "we need to go visit Ursula. If anyone knows why these specific hubs are being attacked, she would."

"Maybe she's run into the golem?" I asked. "Her hammer looks made for golem crushing."

"I sincerely hope she hasn't," Monty said, seriously. "She's a null and may be safe from the siphoning and the

Earth's Breath, but she's not immune from a stone fist crushing her to death."

"It's great to see your cheery optimistic side come out in these situations."

Monty grabbed his cup and headed for the door.

"I'm a mage," Monty said, opening the door. "We don't have a cheery optimistic side. Let's go."

I was about to leave Peaches, the Sprawl Master, on the sofa when he appeared next to me.

<*I didn't want to wake you. You looked pretty comfortable.*>

<*Are you going to see the cold girl?*>

<*Yes, Monty has some questions for her. Did you want to join us?*>

<*Will her guardian be there?*>

<*Yes, especially after what happened earlier. I'm sure Rags will be staying extra close to Cece.*>

<*Then it's only proper I join you—as your bondmate it's very important I stay extra close to you, also. Are you bringing her meat? Should I bring her meat?*>

<*I'm not going over there to see Rags. In fact, I don't need to go over there at all. This is all mage business. Monty is going to ask Cece to look at some runes—which, since I'm not a mage, I really can't decipher.*>

For a brief second he looked dejected—well, as dejected—as a gleaming, red—eyed, mouth-full-of-sharp fangs, hellhound could look. Until he found another angle.

<*The mage is going to the cold girl?*>

<*I just said that. Are you still sleeping?*>

<*It may not be safe. Her power can escape her control. You can't leave him alone.*>

I saw where this was going.

<And you can't leave me alone, on account of us being bond-mates...right?>

<Exactly. See, your thinking is becoming elevators, too.>

<C'mon, then.>

We headed down the hallway and caught up with Monty knocking on Cece's door. A young woman opened the door. She didn't look a day over sixteen, and wore her black hair short and spiky. She gazed down at Peaches, unfazed, as she stepped to one side to let us in.

"What happened to the nanny?" I asked as the young woman placed her hands together and bowed in greeting. "Who's this?"

"In light of the earlier events today, I've taken steps to contain our young ice mage in our absence," Monty said, returning the bow. "This is Viana, of the White Phoenix, Quan's apprentice."

"Welcome, Mr. Montague, Mr. Strong," Viana said as she turned and headed into the apartment. "You wish to see Cece?"

I returned the bow, slightly surprised Monty would place Cece with a teenager. Even if she was Quan's apprentice.

"Please," Monty said. "Only for a moment."

"She's in the back. Follow me, please."

An intricate tattoo of interwoven designs, similar to Quan's, covered half of her face. The subtle turquoise glow highlighting her tan skin was a clear indicator that the design possessed magical properties.

A simple, gray robe, tied at the waist with a white sash, covered her slight frame. The sash was interlinked with metal sections, which blended into the tail of a white phoenix. The design snaked itself around her waist, up over one shoulder and across her chest. Beneath the robe, she wore a black T-shirt, black jeans and a pair of black Chuck Taylors.

"She looks and dresses like some emo teenager," I said, keeping my voice low as Viana led us into the apartment. "You couldn't get Quan? So, we settled for teenage Quan lite?"

"Quan is otherwise occupied after the incident with the grail, and will be for some time," Monty answered, giving me the *stop being rude* look. "Viana is the only one out of one hundred apprentices to pass Quan's acceptance examination. She may look young, but she's probably older than you."

I shuddered at the word "examination" and looked at Viana with a newfound respect. Quan belonged to the White Phoenix: a sect, like Monty's Golden Circle, that trained mages.

However, whereas the Golden Circle specialized in battlemages, the White Phoenix was a sect focused on healing, and training mages in the discipline of restorative arts.

I think Quan interned with the Elders at the Golden Circle at some point, because the restorative part of her discipline usually appeared after she did some serious ass-kicking. I learned pretty quickly that her being a healer didn't mean she couldn't fight. It only meant she knew where to hit you to break the delicate bits, before she healed the agony.

If Viana was Quan's apprentice, it meant she was formidable. If Monty chose her to watch Cece, a Jotnar ice mage that had almost sent The Moscow into a deep freeze, then she was powerful.

But the real test would be if she could survive a hellhound's greeting.

"She's in the back room with her guardian," Viana said, motioning with a hand. "Right that way."

"Thank you," Monty said. "This shouldn't take long."

Viana stood off to the side as Monty headed to the backroom.

<Are we letting the angry man go on alone? It may be dangerous.>

<You're right, but let's watch our manners first, yes?>

<I have. I haven't bitten the bird girl in dark colors.>

<Don't be rude. Say hello to Cece's new nanny. Her name is Viana, and don't forget to smile.>

<Are you sure? You said no one likes it when I smile.>

<Most people just don't understand the depth of your smile. Try extra hard this time. Maybe she'll make you a sausage?>

<Really? You think so?>

I nodded.

<Pretty positive. I mean, who can resist a hellhound smile?>

<I agree, but most people who see my smile, scream first, then run away.>

<It's probably too much smile for them to handle. How often do people see a hellhound?>

<This is true. Frank says I'm a unique specimen.>

<For once, Frank and I agree on something. Go say hello. Don't forget to add a bit of a growl.>

Peaches padded over to where Viana stood and bared his teeth in his most ferocious hellhound smile and growled at her.

TWENTY

Viana looked down and then gazed in my direction.

"Is he trying to say hello?" she asked, raising an eyebrow. "Or is this the slowest attacking hellhound on the planet?"

"He's trying to be friendly," I said, impressed at her composure. "He doesn't have the hang of it quite yet."

"Miss Quan told me all about you," Viana said, crouching down and scratching Peaches behind the ears. He folded like a cheap lawn chair. "I bet he's hungry. Quan said he likes sausages. Do you want a sausage?"

Peaches gave off a low rumble in a perfect imitation of the Dark Goat's engine.

< Tell her yes. Tell her my bondmate is starving me.>

< You keep lying, I'll tell her to make you a healthy sausage.>

He turned to face me with a whine.

< Why do you want to break my stomach?>

"Can you communicate with him, really?" Viana asked. "That's pretty awesome."

"It only sounds awesome if your favorite topic is meat,

trust me. Can you give him"—more whining—"...one sausage? That would be great."

"I can make more if you need," Viana answered and began gesturing. "It's not that hard a cast."

Peaches gave me some side eye.

<For some. Maybe you can have her teach you how to make real meat.>

<I'm not a mage, and do you want this sausage or not?>

<Yes, please. I'm starving.>

I held up a finger.

"One, please."

Viana finished gesturing and produced a large sausage, placing it on the floor in front of Peaches. He gently hovered over it before inhaling the sausage into the bottomless depths of his digestive system.

"Guess he was hungry?"

"No," I said, nudging my shameless ever-hungry hellhound forward. "His default setting is on devour."

"Oh, I see," she answered. "Must be because he's a puppy?"

"Not really," I said, moving around my ever-widening bondmate. "He just thinks if he isn't eating every moment, he must be starving."

"Oh, well, it was nice to meet you," Viana said, stepping out of Peaches' way. "He's cute—I mean, for a hellhound."

"Don't inflate his oversized ego, please," I answered, moving down the hallway to the backroom after Monty. I looked down at Peaches. "Don't forget to say thank you—gently."

Peaches turned and let out a small bark which reverberated through the apartment.

"That's some bark," Viana said, rubbing an ear. "You're welcome, Peaches. Anytime you need a sausage, let me know."

<Did you hear that? She called me cute. Do you think I could get the cold girl's guardian to call me cute?>

<Don't see it happening any time soon. Rags is obviously immune to your hellhound charms.>

<I know, but I don't understand. The bird girl said she would make me meat anytime. That is excellent.>

<She didn't mean that literally.>

<She said "any time." Which means when I'm hungry, I'm going to visit her. Plus, she thinks I'm cute.>

<Let's go see what Monty is doing. I'm sure Rags is just waiting to see you.>

<You think so?>

<Not really. Whatever you do, don't smile at her. She won't think it's cute.>

<I should have saved half of the meat to give to the beautiful guardian.>

<Amazing.>

<That the guardian is beautiful?>

<That you would even consider saving half a sausage to share with Rags.>

<The guardian and I are meant to be together. She is beautiful and I am a cute hellhound. I don't understand—how can she resist my cuteness?>

<Truly, it's a mystery.>

<Can you resist my cuteness?>

<As your bondmate, I don't think your cuteness applies to me. But I can objectively say, for a hellhound, you're pretty up there in the cute department.>

<I think so. I think the beautiful guardian just needs more meat. Can you have the bird girl make her some meat later?>

<I'll ask her later. Let's go see what Monty is up to.>

I shook my head as he padded on ahead of me in confused silence. We got to the back room where Monty was speaking with Cece. Off to the side, sitting next to Cece, was Rags.

Monty was tracing some white symbols in the air. I recognized some of them from Ziller's image of the Earth's Breath.

"I have an exercise for you, Cecelia. This time I want you to try and create a shortcut."

"Are you sure? You asked me not to do that any more," Cece said warily. "Aunt Olga will get really angry if I freeze her building again."

"That's why Viana is here," Monty said, quietly. "To make sure we don't freeze the building again."

I looked back to see Viana standing in the doorway, focused intently on Cece.

"Okay, Mr. Montague," Cece answered, rubbing Rags' neck. "If you promise Aunt Olga won't get upset."

"I promise," Monty answered with a slight smile. "Now, I'm going to trace some symbols. I want you to look for the connection."

"Look for the connection, got it."

"Can you read these?" Monty asked, tracing the symbols slowly. "Do you know what they say?"

"Not really, Mr. Montague," Cece answered. "They look all inside out."

"Inside out? Of course." More gesturing again. Monty now had a string of six runic symbols floating on one line, in front of Cece. "And now? Can you read them now?"

"Yes, I can feel them, but I don't know what they mean," Cece answered. "Is that okay?"

Monty nodded. "That can work. Feeling is how we all start."

"You want me to make a shortcut?"

"Yes. More importantly, can you find a shortcut from this symbol"—he pointed to the first symbol on the left —"to this one?" he finished, pointing to the last symbol on the right. "Look closely."

Cece scrunched her face together and narrowed her eyes at the symbols, then started tracing symbols of her own. She made connecting blue lines between the runes Monty had traced and her new ones. This was like watching Ziller's theories in 3D.

"Can I add some and switch the places?" she asked, still creating more blue lines of energy, overlapping Monty's white ones. "Is that okay? I think I can feel them better now."

"Do you mean switch the order?" Monty asked. "I'm afraid not, they need to be in a—"

"Not switch the order," Cece explained, tracing out two new symbols in her blue energy. "I mean switch the places, like this."

The new symbols were duplicates of the first and last symbols on Monty's line. She placed three symbols facing each other with the last one on the bottom. then repeated the configuration on the outside.

With one last gesture, the runic symbols became solid faces, creating a triangular pyramid inside a larger triangular pyramid. The outer one was a light blue, the inner one a deep blue.

Monty rubbed his chin and stared at the image for a

good ten seconds before saying anything. He shook his head slowly and looked at the floating image from every angle. I sensed the latent energy that pulsed from the symbols.

"Did she get it?" I asked, pointing at the pyramid figure floating in the air. "Whatever that is, it looks powerful."

"Dual tetrahedrons?" Monty said, narrowing his eyes. "How did you do this?"

"I feel them," Cece answered. "Your symbols reminded me of ice. So I stacked them, like crystals."

"That makes perfect sense," Monty said, mostly to himself. "You're an ice mage. It informs how you cast, of course."

"Did I make the shortcut you wanted?" Cece asked, looking for approval. "Was it right?"

"Cecelia, you have done exceedingly well," Monty said with an almost smile. He reached out and was about to pat her on the head, then changed his mind at the last second, and patted her on the shoulder. "I am impressed. Well done."

Cece beamed with excitement, clearly fighting hard to contain herself. Even I was surprised. This was the warmest I'd seen Monty. He'd even given her a compliment which was quite a feat, since he belonged to Master Yat's school of physical complimenting.

"Does this mean I don't have to do homework this week?" Cece asked, clearly influenced by Frank's philosophy of *how to manipulate to get what you want*, except she didn't count on one thing: mages don't bargain.

"Absolutely not," Monty said, and Cece's face fell from the heights of exultation to the depths of despair, or in her case, homework. "You will keep working this shortcut until you can do it with the symbols in every and any order. The tetrahedrons must not collapse, and must be able to be inverted without catastrophic side effects."

"That sounds hard," Cece moaned, sounding like a ten-year-old who had just been given extra chores. "That will take forever, Mr. Montague."

"Then, you better get started right away," Monty said. "Viana will keep a careful eye on you"—he glanced over and nodded at Viana, who returned the nod—"to make sure you stay focused and under control."

My phone rang in my pocket. I checked the number—Ramirez. If he was calling me now, so soon after we spoke, it was bad news. I headed into the other room to take the call.

TWENTY-ONE

I connected the call and was greeted by the sounds of explosions and gunfire

"Angel, what the hell is going on?"

"No time to explain, Strong. You and your mage need to get downtown—now. Shit!" Ramirez yelled. "Get your asses away from that thing now!"

"Golem?" I asked, poking my head back into the room and getting Monty's attention with a wave. "Do you see it?"

"Keep her safe," Monty said to Viana and followed me out of Cece's apartment. He gave me a look. "The golem?"

I nodded.

<Let's go, boy. Now.>

<Now? I was just about to speak to her.>

I didn't bother answering, and Peaches padded to my side with a low growl.

"Do I see it? Do I see it?" Ramirez scoffed. "That... that...thing is destroying Battery Park City. Get down here, now!"

"Are you close to it?" I asked. "Make sure you keep your people away from it."

"Wow, Strong, that's some grade-A advice right there," he said, his voice grim. "Next, you'll be telling me not to waste my bullets because they won't work on something as solid as granite."

"Well...I was—"

"Forget it," Ramirez snapped. "We are keeping back. Right now, to the normals, it just looks like spontaneous explosions occurring in the area. Those who are sensitive can track through its veil and are keeping everyone out of its way."

"It has a veil?"

"Did I stutter?" Ramirez said with a growl. "Stop wasting time. Your buddies Banjo and Cash are down here too."

I groaned inwardly. Things were bad enough without adding the comfort-food duo to the mix. Worse, if they tried to tangle with the golem, they'd get themselves killed.

"Don't let them get close to it."

"Too late," Ramirez said. "One of them—the tall, bald one...I want to say Bango? tried to do that thing your mage does, and created a ball of fire."

"Did it work?"

"Didn't even make it halfway to the rock monster before it just...fizzed out. The rock thing bounced him with a short trip across the street, courtesy of a backhand to the chest."

I had left Cece's now with Monty and Peaches in tow. I hit the stairwell running and they were keeping pace.

"Shit, is he—?"

"An idiot? Yes, and extremely lucky. He should be dead, don't ask me how he survived. Get your asses down here."

"We're on our way," I said. "Give me five minutes."

"I'll do my best. So far the casualities are minor because we've managed to keep it contained, but that won't last." Ramirez cursed under his breath. "Damn thing is strong. Move, move, move! Hurry, Strong."

"We're on our—"

The call disconnected.

"We need to get down there," I said as we jumped into the Dark Goat, roaring the engine to life and flooring the gas pedal. Peaches gave a low growl from the backseat. "Can you sense it, Monty?"

Monty pulled out the document from his pocket.

"Not yet, I can't," Monty said. "Where is the NYTF engaged?"

"Ramirez said Battery Park City," I answered, swerving onto the West Side Highway and cutting off several cars. "I'm guessing we just follow the explosions?"

"That would be one way, yes," Monty said, looking down at the map. "I need to call Ursula. Do not rush into this, not yet."

"What? Are you insane? Lives are on the line."

"Trust me," Monty said, pressing a button on his phone. "Keep back. Get close, but not too close."

Monty connected the call and routed it through the Dark Goat.

"Tristan," Ursula answered, her voice tight with anger. "Tell me you aren't in Battery Park."

TWENTY-TWO

"Not yet we aren't," Monty said. "Where are you?"

"About five minutes away," Ursula answered. "My team is ten minutes out. This attack caught us off guard. A nexus point is under attack, but it doesn't read like Mourn."

"Mourn?" I asked, avoiding traffic. "What is Mourn?"

"I'll explain it later," Monty said quickly. "Ursula, the golem is a siphon for mages."

"Good thing I'm not a mage, then."

"Precisely," Monty said. "When you engage the golem, Simon and his creature will join you, in addition to two other questionable paranormal investigators."

"Excuse me? I'll be doing what?"

"What do you keep reminding me of?" Monty asked, glancing at me.

"That you need to drink coffee? That we need a vacay...STAT?"

"That *you* are *not* a mage," Monty answered. "This situation is tailor-made—"

"Suicide," I finished for Monty. "Are you crazy? I don't know how to face a golem."

"I just need you to keep it occupied," Monty said, looking at the map of hubs. "Ursula, is there a hub nexus point in Battery Park?"

"Yes, a major hub, NP-1, is down there," she answered. "If we're going to be dancing with this golem thing...where will you be?"

"I'll be looking for whoever is holding its leash," Monty said. "He'll be within three hundred yards and needs line of sight."

"Three hundred yards is plenty of ground to cover."

"Indeed. I'm going to ask you to reposition the golem behind some of the buildings if you can," Monty said. "That should force its handler out into the open. Whatever you do, do not allow the golem to destroy the hub."

"Not while I'm breathing," she said, and I believed her. "The rest of it? Can't promise anything, but I see the plan. Good luck."

She ended the call.

"Two words," I said, weaving through traffic, nearly clipping a taxi cab. "Property damage. We bring this thing near buildings, and the entire Dark Council—not just a battalion—will be after us."

"It can't be helped. If Toson forms an army—an unstoppable army, mind you, there won't be any property left to damage. The Dark Council can piss off if they have a problem with it."

"Piss off?" I asked. "That's going to be our response if they come at us, guns and orbs blazing—piss off?"

"Yes," Monty answered, his voice low and laced with menace. "We do not answer to the Dark Council. We have saved this city countless times and will continue to do so without their permission. If they want a war...they will find out why Montague battlemages were the most feared mages on the battlefield."

"I'd rather avoid a Dark Council-Darth Montague war if we can," I said, wary of the threat in Monty's voice. "If we could focus on preventing the city from being crushed by a large rock monster—that would be great."

"Haven't you been paying attention?" Monty asked, exasperated. "At the very least, Ursula sees the plan."

"She sees the plan?" I asked. "I'm glad *someone* sees the plan, because I sure as hell don't. What is the plan, Monty? Ursula and I are bait?"

"It's quite simple," Monty said, keeping his voice calm, which only creeped me out more. "You, your creature, along with Ursula and your two new friends, will engage the golem."

"That's not a plan—that's the fastest way to get crushed tonight," I snapped. "What about Bungie and Smash? Won't they be siphoned?"

"Bangers' energy signature is negligible to the point of being non-existent," Monty said, dismissing my words with a wave. "He's in greater danger of getting siphoned by vacuuming his carpet. His associate is nearly a normal— only in danger of extreme weight loss by ultimate squashing. Make sure you remind him to move around a bit, though."

"Way to go, Mr. Sympathy. They *could* die, you know. They don't belong out here."

"Precisely."

"I don't understand. What do you mean, 'precisely'? You want them to get squished?"

"Of course not," Monty replied. "But they won't listen to you or me or anyone. I sincerely doubt Ramirez's interview will dissuade them, either."

"So we feed them to the golem?"

"The only way is for them to experience this world firsthand. If they won't listen to reason, they must face the truth."

"They could die."

"Only one of us is immortal here, Simon," Monty said with a sigh. "Any one of us could die facing this creature—even you. They want to be paranormal investigators? Then they have to realize that this isn't a game. Every time we face a threat, the stakes are high—the highest. If they can't or won't accept that, they have no business out here."

He was right. Even being cursed alive was no guarantee I could return from being reduced to particulate matter, not that I was looking to test that theory. What bothered me was that Monty was willing to put them in harm's way, knowing they were ill-equipped to deal with the threat. His reasoning was sound, but his method was questionable. Something was off; I just didn't know what. Maybe we really needed a vacay.

"I'll keep an eye on them and make sure they don't get squished by Rocky," I said. "How are you going to find Toson? Three hundred yards is too much area to cover for one person."

"Depends on where the golem is," Monty said, and pointed. "Pull up there. I'll approach the rest of the way on foot."

I stopped the Dark Goat some distance from the NYTF cordon. Flames and fire illuminated the night sky. The light played off Monty's face as he looked somberly at the devastation. He pulled on the sleeves of his Zegna mageiform suit. I could tell this one was runed to take damage, which meant it was unlikely to survive the encounter with Toson.

"Why don't you just wear combat armor?" I asked. "It would be safer. Maybe not as stylish, but definitely safer."

"It's not just a matter of style, though there is that consideration," Monty answered. "I'm a mage. Combat armor would prevent my mobility. If I can't move freely, I can't fight efficiently. That would result in a rapid visit to Haven, or worse."

"This is going to suck," I said, shaking my head and looking off in the distance at the destruction caused by the golem. "You sure you want to do this part alone?"

"I can't go near the golem yet," Monty said with a nod. "The siphon would only feed it. My best course of action is to confront Toson. If you find yourself in over your head—get them away."

"Where exactly would you like me to take them?"

"Underground, the subway or a tunnel. Anywhere off the surface. It shouldn't be able to follow you."

"Sounds like a plan," I said. "What if Toson is too strong? Professor Ziller said he's close to an Archmage."

"I don't intend on facing him, just getting close enough to use Cecelia's shortcut."

"That sort of sounds like facing him. How close do you need to get?"

"Closer than I want to," Monty said. "Her shortcut requires some proximity. I can boost it, but it will still be dangerously close."

"Still, she figured it out. Was the answer beyond you? Or did you just want to give her something to make her feel better after converting The Moscow into an ice palace?"

"Astute," Monty answered with a nod. "She is a gifted mage. Her solution is elegant and only requires a slight adjustment. It was limited by her focus on the crystalline formations of ice."

"So you knew how to make the shortcut?"

"Every teacher shows the student what they need, not everything the teacher knows," Monty said and started walking off. "Be careful, Simon."

"You too, Monty. Go shut down that mage—I'll deal with Rocky."

He walked off and faded into the night, disappearing with one of his mage camouflages. I pulled up to the NYTF cordon, where I was promptly stopped by a bored-looking officer.

"I'm afraid you're going to have to turn around, sir," the officer instructed in standard checkpoint speech. "This area is closed off and dangerous to the public."

"Sure," I said. "Have you seen the reason you're keeping the public away?"

"I just follow orders. Director said I get overtime by standing here. That's good enough for me."

"Actually, that's not good enough," I said, getting out and opening the rear suicide door. "You need to be on point tonight or innocent people might die."

"Yeah, sure. Who are you, again?"

Peaches stepped out in dramatic hellhound fashion, massive head first, then enormous paws. The officer took a few steps back when Peaches stared at him. He looked from Peaches to the Dark Goat and let his shaky hand rest on the holster of his weapon as the blood slowly drained from his face.

"You don't want to do that—trust me," I said, reaching slowly inside my jacket. I flashed him my ID. "Director Ramirez is waiting for me."

The officer, whose name-tag read, *Landis* grabbed his shoulder radio without taking his eyes off of us.

"I have an unidentified person at the south cordon who says he's here for Director Ramirez," Landis said, his voice cracking ever so slightly. "He's accompanied by a large canine—I think. Over."

"That's Strong," Ramirez's voice barked over the radio. "Let him through."

Landis, now completely alert and semi-ready to bolt, nodded and waved at me to come through the cordon.

<Don't forget to be polite and smile at the officer.>

Peaches bared his fangs with a growl, and Landis backed up several feet.

"Shit!" he said, nearly pulling out his gun. "What kind of creature is that?"

"The kind that will chew your arm off, if you pull out that gun," I said, walking past the cordon. "Keep on your toes, Officer Landis. There are worse things out here tonight."

"Fuck me," I heard the officer say as we kept walking down the street. "That is *not* a dog."

<Did I scare him?>

<Yes, but that fear will probably keep him alive tonight, so good job.>

<Good enough to get an extra sausage?>

<No. Life is not measured in sausages. Besides, you just ate.>

<I deserve an extra sausage because you pulled me away just

before I spoke to the beautiful guardian. I could tell she was thinking I was cute.>

<She was thinking no such thing. Besides, what were you waiting for—an invitation?>

<Well, I did rescue her. It's only fair she talk to me first.>

<Boy, if you want to ever have a chance of being with Rags, let that notion go right now. Next time you see her, bring her a sausage and just talk. Don't wait for her to speak first.>

<Do you think that will work?>

<I'm not an expert, but...>

<True. Your female wants to hurt you. I don't want the beautiful guardian to hurt me. I don't think you are the right person to speak to—even if you are my bondmate.>

<My female wants to hurt me? What are you talking about?>

<Your female, the angry lady, wants to hurt you.>

<How do you know that? You can't possibly know that she...>

<I'm a hellhound and your bondmate. I know who wants to hurt you.>

<Right. Anyway, I'm not taking personal relationship advice from a hellhound. It's not the same.>

<What's not the same?>

<Human relationships and canine relationships—very different.>

<Then, why do you want me to take your advice? We are bondmates, but you aren't a hellhound or a canine.>

I was about to answer, but I didn't have a good response. Peaches the Hellhound Zen Master had outmaneuvered me. I blamed the lizard.

<That's actually a good point.>

<I will ask Frank what he thinks about this.>

<He's not a canine, either.>

<True, but dragons are wise. At least wiser than most humans.>

<Frank is closer to a wiseass, and he's not a dragon. He's a lizard.>

<He is not...>

"Strong!" Ramirez yelled when he saw me. "Get over here!"

<We'll discuss this later.>

TWENTY-THREE

We made our way through the bustle of activity to the command vehicle.

"Took you long enough," Ramirez said, smoothing out a map on the small table. "Where's Tristan?"

Personnel moved around us, managing the cordon and response teams.

"I dropped him off a few blocks away," I said, looking at the map. "He's tackling this—"

"A few blocks away?" Ramirez asked, his voice booming through the vehicle. "The monster is not a few blocks away, it's over here!"

I gave him a look and waited for him to calm down. It usually took a few seconds before he calmed down enough to listen. The command vehicle had become deathly still in response to his outburst.

"Everybody out," I said in a voice that gave no other option. "I need to speak to the Director alone for a few."

Everyone hesitated until Angel gave them a slight nod, at which point they poured out of the vehicle in a rush.

"Strong—" Ramirez started.

"I don't work for the NYTF"—I pointed a finger at his chest—"and neither does Monty or Peaches."

"I know, I'm so—"

"Then, tell me what the hell has you so stressed out that you think screaming at me is going to fix the situation, Angel?"

"It's the job, Strong. I'm sorry I yelled at you. This job has me wound up."

"You've been doing this for years. What are you talking about? You're the best Director the NYTF has had. Your people love you, or at least tolerate you, although, maybe it's just the fear of your big mouth at this point?"

"Hilarious. Maybe you should go tell the rock beast jokes?" Ramirez answered with half a smile. "I care too much." He rubbed his face with one massive hand. "I'm stressed because they're facing creatures no one in their right mind should have to face. I'm seeing NYTF personnel crack under the pressure, quit the force and need years of therapy."

"They knew what they signed up for," I said, remembering Monty's earlier words about Bangers and Mash. "You didn't force them to join the NYTF."

"Doesn't change the fact that this job...it breaks you. Small cracks at first. You see things you think are impossible, day after day, until it becomes normal—then one day, you see something that blows all that away and you begin to question your sanity, or think you need to take matters into your own hands, like Rott did."

"Rott also lost Cassandra. That's what pushed him over the edge."

"He was on the edge long before the Lieutenant checked out. She was just the final straw."

"Are you okay?" I asked, concerned. "Do you need to take some time off? Do you feel yourself cracking?"

"Do I sound like I need to take some time off?" Ramirez growled, pounding the table. "I only feel like I'm cracking when I have to deal with you and your people."

"You do sound a little tightly wound up," I said. "How are those bowel movements? Maybe what you need is a laxa—"

"What I *need*, is for you and your MIA mage to stop that rock thing out there from putting my people and city in danger. That's what I need."

"Right, that, and a large dose of valium—extra chill."

"Do not push me, Strong. Tonight is not the night."

"You sound like the irritable pain in the ass you've always been," I said, looking at the map again. "Maybe we all just need a vacation from the madness."

"Vacation? I won't hold my breath."

Another explosion rocked through the night.

"I hear the destruction, but where is it?"

Ramirez turned to look out of the command vehicle.

"Stop loitering and get back to work!" Ramirez yelled. "We have a creature to contain. Make sure the area is clear of normals, and I want roadblocks for a mile in both directions. No one gets in."

His people poured back into the command vehicle.

"I can see why they love you," I said, watching them execute the orders. "Must be that smooth motivational management style you have."

"Shove it, Strong. Tell me what you're going to do."

"Right now? Hope that thing didn't hear your big

mouth and come crush us," I said, rubbing my ear. "Show me where Rocky is."

He put a large sausage of a finger on the map.

"There," Ramirez said. "That thing is right there, for now. Nothing we've thrown at it has worked or even slowed it down."

"I'm expecting someone. When she gets here, tell your men to let her through and pull your people back. I don't want them getting hurt—or worse."

"Does she know what's she's doing? Is she a mage?"

"She's qualified, trust me. Where's Bangers and Mash?"

"Central EMTe bus," Ramirez pointed to the blue ambulance near the command vehicle. It was the one closest to the main command. There were three more of the same in the area, in addition to other NYTF first responder vehicles. "Frank is with them."

"He's still working?" I asked. "I thought he'd be retired by now."

"He said he couldn't retire while your agency still operated in the city," Ramirez said. "Something about being the only thing that stood against a menace to society and complete Armageddon."

"Everyone is a comedian," I said, leaving Ramirez and the command vehicle. "Get your people back now. My backup should be here any second. I'm going to go check on the rookies."

"You heard the man," Ramirez boomed. "Pull our people back."

EMTe stood for *EMT elite*. The NYTF used these paramedics whenever they encountered some kind of supernatural disaster, or when Monty was allowed to run rampant, which in their opinion was pretty much the same thing these days, especially after our last run in with the Dark Council Enforcers.

The medics all wore dark-red uniforms and drove around in extra-large, blue, rune-covered ambulances. I had the utmost respect for them—they were the Navy Seals of the paramedics.

The veterans, which in the EMTe meant anyone lasting longer than a year, were tough as two-day-old steak and were willing to risk their lives, no matter the situation. Some of them had magical healing abilities, and all of them possessed a certain sensitivity to supernatural phenomena.

In the back of the central bus, I saw Frank, working on Bangers.

Frank defined grizzled: older, mid-sixties, built like a wall and probably as tough. He was the oldest EMTe still in the field and was affectionately known as the OG. I'd thought that meant "old gangsta", but one of the other EMTe medics informed me it meant "original geezer."

Next to Bangers, I saw Mash, freshly bandaged from his run-in with the golem. They were not having a good night.

"Hey, Frank," I said, peeking into the bus. "What's shaking?"

"Knew it was only a matter of time before I saw your ugly face," Frank answered without looking up. "How was the land of the rising sun?"

"Painful," I said, giving Bangers and Mash the once over. "What happened to these two?"

"These two rocket scientists decided to tangle with that thing—and lost," Frank said around an unlit cigar. "This one is lucky to be alive. If he hadn't been wearing that"—Frank pointed to a heavy-duty Kevlar vest that had been shredded—"we'd be reading last rites right about now."

"Are you saying they're unfit to face that thing?"

"Unfit?" Frank said. "No, no, I'm not saying they're unfit."

Bangers looked at me with a smug expression as if to say: *See? Even the medic thinks we can do this. Take that!* At least he had the mage arrogance down pat.

"Go on," I said, raising a finger, knowing Frank was just getting started. "What's the prognosis?"

"These two asshats need to be on the first bus to Haven. It's not that they're unfit—they're suicidal," Frank spat. "This one"—he pointed to Bangers—"rushed the rock thing with the equivalent of a lit match. His partner, Einstein over there, instead of running for cover, decided to back him up. That rock thing nearly crushed the stupidity out of both of them tonight."

"Which bus is next?" I asked, observing Bangers and Mash. "The next one out?"

"This one," Frank said. "I'm driving, and we're out in two minutes."

"Got it," I said. "Let me have a word with them."

"Good luck. They wanted me to patch them up so they could go back out to their funeral," Frank said. "Pair of idiots if you ask me. Two minutes, Strong."

Frank stormed off. He sounded upset, but I'd known him long enough to understand that his anger was really out of concern for Bangers and Mash. He didn't want them to throw their lives away, and if I had anything to do with it, they wouldn't. First, though, we were going to get to the truth.

"Let's make this brief, because we don't have time," I said, looking at Bangers. "There's no way you studied in the Golden Circle. Hell, I doubt you even know where it is."

"How dare you question my—" Bangers started.

"I'm not done," I said, cutting him off. "I'm sure you mean well, but all you're going to do tonight is die—and take your associate with you. And you"—I said, looking at Mash—"ex-Navy Seal my ass. Don't even try to deny it. No self-respecting Frogman would partner up with a pretend mage."

"I am a mage," Bangers admitted. "I never trained at the Golden Circle and never got past basic casting, but I am a mage...an apprentice, really."

"And you?" I said, looking at Mash. "What's your story?"

"Mess," Mash said. "I worked with Navy Seals...in the mess hall."

"You're a cook?"

"I fed the Navy Seals."

"You realize feeding Navy Seals doesn't make you one? Not even close?"

Mash nodded, embarrassed.

"I have to say, you two have to be the most fearless pair of clowns I've ever encountered," I said, shaking my head. "Your mission is over—right now."

"What makes you so qualified to face the creature?" Bangers asked, indignantly. "What makes you think you can face it?"

"A valid question—one which I will indulge, because well...because I don't want to see you two as bloody smears on the streets of my city."

I extended my arm and let the silvery mist extend from my hand, forming Ebonsoul a second later. They both looked on in shock.

"Is that all—you can summon a knife?" Bangers asked, the surprise evident in his voice. "I'm not impressed."

I pulled up a sleeve and ran Ebonsoul gently across my forearm, creating a large gash.

"What are you doing?" Mash said, concerned. "Robert, get the medic!"

"How?" Bangers asked when he started seeing the wound heal itself. "You're not a mage."

Mash opened his eyes wide. "How did you do that?"

Frank reappeared at the rear of the bus.

"Did you convince them?" Frank asked. "Or do I need to"—he cracked his knuckles—"use my sedative?"

I jumped out of the bus.

"I think they understand now," I said, rolling down my sleeve. "Tell Roxanne to keep them on lock-down until this situation is resolved. I don't want them getting caught in the middle of a rock and a hard place."

"Got it," Frank said, closing the rear doors on the still shocked Bangers and Mash. "They mean well. They just don't know what they don't know, which will get them dusted out here."

I nodded as I heard a car come to a skidding halt, just outside the cordon.

"That's my backup," I said. "You take care of yourself, old man."

"Look who's talking. You're probably older than me."

"You know too much, OG."

"Ain't that the truth," Frank answered with a wink,

chewing his cigar. "Go do what you need to do. Don't get dead."

"That's the plan. Make sure Roxanne keeps those two in Haven for a few days."

"I'm sure she will. You watch yourself out there."

Frank jumped into the cab of the bus, started the engine and turned on the lights as he sped out of the area.

Ursula walked up to me a second later, her arm covered in a silver mist. She was about to materialize her weapon.

"You ready for this?" she asked.

"Not really," I said, switching out my magazine for entropy rounds. "Never stopped me before."

"I hope you have something stronger than bullets."

"Don't worry," I said, holstering Grim Whisper. "I'm just full of surprises."

"That's what I'm afraid of."

TWENTY-FOUR

We headed to the location Ramirez had indicated on the map.

"Which direction did Tristan go?" Ursula asked, materializing her hammer as we closed on the golem. "The nexus point is over there."

I glanced over at Ursula, who led the Decons and Magical Nulls—Elite Division, or DAMNED. It was a team made up of a group of Weres.

This was the group tasked with safeguarding the city's nexus points, maintaining the balance of runic energy to prevent destabilization, and removing any potentially lethal residual traces.

They were the first and last line of defense when it came to maintaining the network of points intact. Ursula, who was a werebear, was a tall, heavyset woman with short black hair, and the physique to match any Olympic power-lifter. Tonight, she was wearing a black dragonscale T-shirt, jeans, and combat boots.

Down the length of one arm, the intricate pattern of

runes gave off a dull golden light. Her presence commanded respect, which was due in part to the massive, rune-covered hammer she held in one hand, hefting it without any measurable effort.

"I dropped him off north of here. I'm guessing he's going to approach the golem and then circle around to find the mage controlling it."

"And we're going to play tag with it," Ursula said with a smile. "This is going to be interesting."

"Listen," I said, raising a hand. "I understand this may be hammer time for you, but I'm not looking to get pancaked tonight. We stop this thing, or at least distract it from destroying your nexus point; but if it gets dicey, we pull back and regroup."

"No," Ursula said. "My responsibility is to the nexus points and keeping them intact. If even one is destroyed, the integrity of the entire network is compromised. That is a bad thing—stuff of your worst nightmares bad. If you need to cut and run, I get it. I'm pretty the hellhound and I can do what needs to be done."

"First off, I don't 'cut and run' unless a strategic retreat is required, in which case, staying alive to fight another day is a sound strategy. Second, Peaches stays with me. If I go, he goes...with me."

"Makes sense," she said with a wide grin. "Someone has to keep the immortal safe, I guess."

"You're worse than Monty," I said. "No one has to keep me safe. All I'm saying is let's not rush into this without thinking."

"Relax, Strong," Ursula said. "I'm just yanking your chain. I'm serious about the points, though. I won't...can't abandon a point in danger of being destroyed, so we better make sure this thing doesn't get close to the nexus point."

"Understood," I said, "We'll keep it safe."

"Good," she said, looking down at Peaches. "Will he be okay?"

"Peaches is nearly indestructible, but I'm not playing tag with anything tonight. We get its attention and pull it behind a building if possible, to give Monty a chance to find the mage—if not, we get the hell out of Dodge."

"I'm not letting it destroy a nexus point," Ursula said, her smile gone. "If it manages that, we're going to have worse things than a golem to deal with—trust me on that."

"Where exactly is this hub, just so I know where to do my Gandalf Balrog move?"

"Your what?" Ursula asked, looking at me like I had grown an extra head. "Can you say that in English?"

"You know, 'You…Shall Not…pass'?" I asked, spreading out my arms in my best imitation of Gandalf blocking the Balrog. *The Fellowship of the Ring*? You've never read Tolkien?"

"Who?" Ursula asked. "Is he joining us tonight? Because from the feel of this thing, we may be here a while."

"I can't believe you've never read—never mind. If we get through this, I'll make sure to fix that. Where is the hub?"

"Bowling Green. The structure is somewhat in-between like all nexus points, but it connects to our plane at Bowling Green, not far from here."

"Got it, we can't let it get to Bowling Green."

"Is this Tolkien person joining us?" Ursula asked. "Because I'm sensing a serious energy signature."

"Only in spirit," I said. "This one is all us tonight. Well, us and your team, of course—how many did you say were on your team?"

"Two more."

"Two more what? Two dozen, two hundred?"

"Two," she held up two fingers. "Just two more."

"Me, Monty, Peaches, and you and your team of three," I said. "Against an unstoppable rock thing and a psycho mage?"

Ursula nodded with a grin. "Nothing is unstoppable." She turned in the direction of the golem. "I almost feel sorry for them."

The roar of another explosion filled the area, followed by the roar of the golem. I think I preferred the explosion. We were standing near South Cove Park, a few blocks away from where the World Trade Center once stood. and in the center of the park, moving toward West Street, was what I could only describe as a giant man-shaped rock creature.

Cracks ran along its body, revealing lines of what looked like magma, making its skin resemble an active volcano. It stood nearly twenty feet tall and was attempting to crush the NYTF who were dousing it with water and chemical solutions created to stop fires.

All that did was create steam and limit visibility. Another NYTF group tried to contain it with shoulder-mounted rocket launchers, and I watched a volley of rockets sail into the golem and explode with no effect. They might as well have been throwing cotton balls at it.

The golem roared again.

"That's our cue," I said, moving closer and drawing

Grim Whisper. "Let's see if we can get its attention, at least."

I unloaded the magazine. The entropy rounds punched holes into the golem's body, causing it to turn and focus on me with another roar.

"Good job," Ursula said with a nod, swinging her hammer. "Looks like you got its attention."

"You plan on using that oversized paperweight? Or is it just for show?"

Electric arcs raced across the hammer's surface and up her arm. I gave her some space in case she needed to discharge some excess electricity.

"Kirves isn't for show," she said, running at the golem. "Stay back."

"I still can't believe she calls that thing Curvy."

<Can I go bite the rock man?>

<No. Biting means getting close, and I don't want that thing to swat you like it did Bangers. I think you're going to need to go XL on that thing.>

<XL? Do you mean get big?>

<That's what XL means—extra large.>

<Why don't you just say extra large? Are you saying I'm fat? Is that why you want me on an exercise program?>

<Can we discuss that later, when we don't have a large rock creature about to squash us?>

<Going XL means my sausage needs to be XL, too. I think it's only fair.>

Peaches bowed his head and growled. The runes along his flanks exploded with red light as the air around him became charged with energy. He shook his body, spread his legs, and barked—a real bark that left my ears ringing.

The sound deafened me for a few seconds as all of the

windows in the surrounding buildings and vehicles shattered. Peaches increased in size, reaching XL status.

<Hit it with your omega beams. Blast it to bits!>

I pointed at the golem.

<MY BALEFUL GLARE DOES NOT POSSESS THE NECESSARY POWER TO RENDER THE CREATURE DOWN TO ITS COMPONENT PARTS.>

<Can you hit it hard enough to stagger, then?>

<THIS IS A VIABLE OPTION. HOWEVER, THE CHANCE OF THE WERE-CREATURE ENGAGING THE GOLEM BEING IN DANGER MAKES THIS COURSE OF ACTION PROHIBITIVE.>

<Fine, find a firing solution and blast it when you can. I'll get Ursula out of the way.>

I ran to Ursula, and had almost reached her, when a boulder crashed into the ground next to me. I looked in the sky behind me and saw a comet streaking my way, except this comet was decidedly human-shaped. It took me a few seconds to realize that it wasn't a comet.

It was Monty.

TWENTY-FIVE

I was momentarily distracted from Monty's blazing flight by several large, orange orbs racing through the night sky, heading in the direction of the hub.

<Get Monty! He's hurt.>

Peaches turned his head, focused on Monty and blinked out. One moment a massive hellhound the size of a large SUV was standing next to me, and the next he was mid-air catching Monty in his large maw and dousing the flames. I really hoped he didn't think Monty was a sausage.

Peaches disappeared from sight again and appeared next to me, placing a slightly charbroiled Monty on the ground, who groaned as he got to his feet.

"That certainly gives a new meaning to 'coming in hot'," Monty said, shaking off some of the excess drool from his ruined jacket. "Please thank your creature for the assist. It would have been an unpleasant landing had he not intercepted my trajectory."

<I BELIEVE THAT ACT DESERVES ADDI-

TIONAL PROTEIN IN THE FORM OF LARGE
PORTIONS OF MEAT.>

*<Give him a chance to recover. He was just blasted across the
city. I'm sure he'll make you some meat. Thank you for catching
him.>*

I patted PeachesXL on the flank, still in awe that he
was a puppy.

<YOU ARE MOST WELCOME, BONDMATE. I
SENSE AN ANTAGONISTIC FORCE HEADED IN
OUR DIRECTION. WOULD YOU LIKE ME TO
ENGAGE, OR CONFRONT THE GOLEM
CURRENTLY HEADING AWAY FROM OUR
POSITION?>

<Shit! You can't let the golem get close to the hub!>

<I DO NOT UNDERSTAND. WHY DOES FECAL
MATTER FACTOR IN TO THIS ENGAGEMENT?>

*<It doesn't! It's just an expression. Please go help Ursula stop
the golem. We'll stop the mage coming our way.>*

<AS YOU WISH.>

He bounded off to intercept the golem, who was
currently being given shock therapy by Ursula and her
hammer. I made a mental note never to get on her bad
side as she pounded the golem and sent bolts of electricity
at it.

"What happened?" I asked a disheveled Monty. "Were
you able to use the shortcut?"

He shook his head and threw his jacket to one side.

"Ruined," he said with disgust. "That was bespoke."

"I'd really suggest combat armor. Maybe Ermenegildo
can start the Montague Battlemage Collection?"

"It appears the Earth's Breath has afforded Toson
mastery over more than just the earth discipline," Monty

said, glancing back at the jacket. "I really *liked* that jacket."

"That *was* a nice jacket," I said, glancing at what was left of the smoldering jacket."Looks like Toson got the hang of fire, too."

"Indeed. It was all I could do to prevent myself being incinerated where I stood. His control is impressive."

"I noticed what looked like orbs of destruction accompanying your flight," I said, glancing skyward. "They headed that way, toward the hub."

"Most likely Toson trying to finish the job," Monty answered, gazing in the direction of the hub. "I'm not seeing any activity over there, besides your creature and Ursula."

"And Toson is headed this way?" I asked, looking over to where Ursula and Peaches were tangling with the golem. "I don't know how long they can keep that up."

Monty glanced over. "We can't let the golem reach the hub. Once Toson arrives, I'm going to need you to distract him while I cast the shortcut."

"Why does 'distract him' sound like 'be a moving target' while he tries to blast me?"

"Speaking of moving targets, where are Bangers and Mash?" Monty asked, looking around. "Don't tell me—?"

"No, I sent them to Haven before they were the ones bangersmashed. Turns out Bangers is a mage apprentice dropout."

"A weak one, if you ask me. What about Mash?"

"Mash is an ex-military cook. The only time he dealt with Navy Seals was when he was feeding them. I told Frank they needed to be put on lockdown, just in case."

"Charlatans—how they've survived this long is a miracle," Monty said. "I'm sure Roxanne will want to hold them for 'observation' if only to keep them out of trouble."

"What's the plan?" I asked, reloading Grim Whisper. "My magic missile isn't going to do squat against someone who flambéed you, and getting close enough to use Ebonsoul doesn't look likely."

"I'm not asking you to engage Toson in combat. He may be beyond both our abilities," Monty replied. "I just need you to push his buttons and distract him, enrage him if possible. Remember, he needs to keep most of his energy and focus on the golem. Splitting that focus will give us an opening."

"You want me to piss-off the super-powerful mage coming to destroy us?"

"Yes," Monty said. "It seems to be something you are supremely adept at."

"Why don't we call in the big guns? Starting with Dex."

"In case you haven't realized," Monty said, gesturing and forming violet orbs all around us, "tonight, we *are* the big guns."

"I'm not quite feeling the 'big gun' vibe. Big target maybe, but definitely not big gun."

"It would seem...there's no time," Monty said, looking up. "We have incoming."

I looked up and saw Toson. He reminded me of an angry Liam Neeson and, for a brief second, I wondered if he was going to threaten us with his "particular set of skills". I noticed the glowing Earth's Breath around his neck, as he glanced in the distance to where the golem was currently doing the rock-crushing tango with Ursula and Peaches.

Toson wore a brown robe similar to Jen's, though his was covered with red and yellow runes that danced around as it blew in the wind. He was standing on a large flame-covered boulder, one that floated in our direction.

"Monty, he's riding a flaming boulder."

"Yes, I'm aware. I did mention he's an elemental mage?"

"A flaming boulder. I will give him style points for that one," I said under my breath. "Are you ready? How long do you need?"

Monty cast a camouflage rune and disappeared from view. He began inscribing symbols into the ground. Even his energy signature was masked. I could barely sense him.

"He'll see through this once he's in proximity," Monty said. "By the time he does, I should have the cast complete, and the shortcut will shut down the artifact."

"How long are we talking, here? He looks like the type to blast first and ask later."

"I need him completely focused on you," Monty said. "Thirty seconds should suffice. I have the rest primed for the cast."

"Thirty seconds, got it," I said, starting my mental timer as I ran forward to intercept Toson. "Time to try some diplomacy."

"Who are *you*?" Toson asked as he gently landed the blazing boulder in front of me. "Stand aside."

"Can't do that," I said. "I'm going to have to ask you to cease and desist."

"Excuse me? Cease and desist? Who *are* you?"

"I'm going to guess you are the owner of the unauthorized golem," I said blithely, glancing over at where the golem was trying to crush Ursula and Peaches. "I'm going to need you to unsummon said golem and leave the city. This is your one and only warning."

Toson narrowed his eyes and looked down his nose at me—the usual mage expression. I made sure I had my mala bracelet free.

"Are you mad?" Toson asked as his hands burst into flames. Large chunks of stone broke from the earth and started floating lazily around him. "You're not even a mage. Do you know who I am?"

"Let me guess," I said. "You feel your rightful place is being usurped and because you weren't being listened to and no one on the Red Mountain bowed to your every whim, you, like a spoiled brat, stole that"—I pointed to the Earth's Breath—"summoned that"—I pointed to the golem without taking my eyes off of Toson—"and proceeded to think you could just take whatever you wanted. That about right?"

I could practically see his blood pressure rise. Mage goading—it was just too easy. I caught the motion of the stones first, and pressed the mala bead, materializing my shield just in time to deflect a medium-sized stone, one the size of my head, from slamming into me.

The impact catapulted me back. I landed in a roll and drew Grim Whisper, firing. The rounds never reached him, crashing into the floating stones, which now whirled around him, effectively shielding him.

"You're with that mage, aren't you? You two were the best Orahjene could find to defend her cause?" Toson scoffed. "Where is she? Even with a shift, she is weaker than me. Is she so frightened to face me herself that she would send incompetents to their death in her stead?"

"Actually, she said she had a spa appointment she

couldn't break and wondered if we could handle—what did she call you?—a minor nuisance, in her absence."

"Minor nuisance? *I* am the rightful First Elder of the Red Mountain," Toson said, raising his voice. "How dare you meddle in affairs that do not concern you!"

"Because, unlike you, Jen asked nicely—and you, I'm discovering, are a second-rate, mage apprentice, hack."

"Jen?" Toson asked, seemingly more upset about that, than my insult. "Her name is Orahjene...not Jen."

"In fact," I continued, ignoring him, "I know a little ice mage girl that has more power in her pinky than you have in your entire body. She doesn't need an artifact or a golem to get things done, either."

"You have no idea the forces you are facing, you insignificant flea of a human!"

Toson raised a fist and I felt the tremor, before noticing the golem had shifted trajectories and was headed my way. I moved back to where Monty had inscribed symbols into the ground.

"I think I have his complete attention now," I said, looking at the infuriated Toson. "Whatever you're going to do—now would be a good time."

Silence.

"Monty?" I said, looking around. "You out there?"

"Did your mage abandon you?" Toson asked as he closed the distance. "I was going to end you with my creature, but I think I will enjoy snuffing out your life personally."

He waved a hand, and the golem turned around with Ursula and Peaches in tow. It plodded slowly back on a trajectory toward Bowling Green and the hub.

I materialized Ebonsoul as Toson approached.

"You're going to find that snuffing part harder than you think."

He paused in his approach. "You have skill," Toson said, materializing a blade of his own. "But your courage will not save you tonight. It is a pity you will not live to see the new era I have set in motion."

"Listen, I can appreciate you want to be a hands-on kind of guy, what with the killing me personally and all, but this is a bad idea. You really want to stop all of this."

"You're scared?" Toson scoffed. "I would be, in your place. I promise you a quick death—a mercy I rarely grant."

"I'm flattered," I said, stepping closer to the symbols Monty inscribed. "Why are you doing this? I mean, really? Why not go out and start another sect? Call yours the Blue Mountain and call it a day."

"Start another sect?" Toson said, stepping into a fighting stance. "My family has been part of the Red Mountain sect for countless generations. I am the rightful successor. My power dwarfs Orahjene's. I am destined to be First Elder. I will turn the Red Mountain into the sect it should be."

I noticed the bare feet as he circled around.

"What's that? A sect of peace, love, and happiness?"

"My world, like yours, only recognizes one thing—power," he said. "I will begin by forming my golem army. Then I will bring all of the sects under one Elder."

"This one Elder—did you nominate yourself?"

"I am the most qualified, the strongest warrior"—he touched the Earth's Breath—"and the leader of the golem army. I know the truth, I have seen it."

I shook my head. "Let me guess, Orahjene disagrees with you."

"She is short-sighted and foolish," Toson answered. "She will be made an example of for her defiance. She could have had it all—with me."

I took a deep breath and stilled my thoughts.

"We don't need to do this," I said, sensing the vibrations around me. "Give back the Earth's Breath and go back to your sect. I'm sure they'd understand. I'm sure she'd understand, probably even forgive you."

"There is no going back. Not now, not ever. Too much has been done that can't be undone."

"I don't want to kill you."

"How ambitious, of you to think you can," Toson scoffed. "I am a blade master. This will be over before you know what happened."

"Bring it."

"Your name, so that I may recall it when your body lies cold on the earth."

"Are you serious?"

"Deadly serious," Toson replied. "I will give you a warrior's death of honor, and will utter your name as you are buried."

"And people say I need to get out more," I muttered. "Strong, Simon Strong."

"Very well, Strong," Toson said, holding his blade to his forehead. "Today was your last sunrise and last sunset. Tonight, you will die a warrior."

"Boy, are you in for a surprise."

TWENTY-SIX

Toson slid forward, leading with his blade. I parried the thrust and dodged to the side. I ducked down the next second, as one of the stone satellites nearly decapitated me.

I kept my shield up and wondered where the hell Monty was when I saw the Earth's Breath start to glow. Toson lunged again, forcing me to backpedal. A plume of flame burst forward from his open hand as I rolled to the side and right into a barrage of marble-sized stones.

I raised the shield to deflect them and realized too late that they were a misdirection. A larger stone sailed along the ground and slammed into my leg sideways, right at the knee, nearly shattering it. I fell to the ground with a groan, holding my leg. My body flushed hot as it repaired the damage.

"That...that was sneaky," I said through clenched teeth, fighting the pain. "I thought you were a blade master?"

"Your first mistake was trying to think," Toson scoffed. "There are no rules in warfare. I am a blade master, and I am also an elemental mage. Both are tools, weapons to be used when prudent and necessary. Especially against an amateur."

Toson approached, apparently confident in the knowledge that the fight was over. I turned, keeping my bent leg between us as I held my knee. I just needed him to take a few more steps. I made sure to keep the groaning going, even after my body had healed.

He stepped close to deliver the final blow with his blade, and I unleashed a strike of my own, kicking the side of his knee and slicing his arm with Ebonsoul. The sick crunch of a break filled the night as he fell back with a yell, shocked I was able to attack at all.

"How did you? How could you?"

A rush of power filled me as Ebonsoul siphoned energy from Toson. His face filled with surprise beneath the pain. I didn't know how to manipulate the earth, but I knew how to fire a magic missile. The power I felt was overwhelming, somehow I knew this wasn't Toson—it was the power of the Earth's Breath inside Toson.

I let the power fill me as he began speaking under his breath. A wall of stone rose from the ground between us, as he unleashed an immense fireball my way. I leapt to the side, extended my arm and let the power within flow.

"*Ignisvitae!*" I yelled, unleashing the power into my arm.

A violet beam blasted the stone wall, punching a hole clear through it. I limped over to the wall, still feeling a bit of pain in my knee and peeked through the smooth hole. Nothing. Toson was gone.

"Shit!" I yelled, slamming the wall. "Where the hell are you, Monty!"

"That was quite exemplary," Monty said, materializing

next to me. "But I think we may have miscalculated; that, or Professor Ziller was wrong."

"Where the hell were you?" I yelled, whirling on him. "Where did you go? You said thirty seconds...thirty seconds!"

"I was here the whole time. I managed to activate the shortcut to no effect, which required I change tactics."

"You changed tactics? To what? Hide and watch me get my ass slammed?"

"As I said," Monty replied calmly, "you were exemplary and in no immediate danger. I did enjoy the drama with the knee, though. That was a nice touch—even if it was a tad overdone. Bravo."

I almost blasted him with a magic missile.

"What the hell, Monty? I could've used the assist."

"No, you couldn't," he said, serious. "We weren't going to stop Toson tonight. You surprised him, but he won't underestimate us again. The next time, he will unleash his full ability."

"What are you saying? He was holding back?"

"We're both still here with all limbs attached, even if mine are mildly scorched. I'd say that's a fair assessment."

"Then what was he doing?"

"If I had to hazard a guess, I'd say gathering intelligence."

"Intelligence? You mean this was a scouting mission?"

"I can't say for certain," Monty answered, looking in the direction of the hub. "In the meantime, we have a golem to stop."

"Dammit, Peaches!" I said, turning to look in the direction of where the golem was. It was gone too. "What the—?"

Peaches had reverted to normal size and was bounding over with Ursula behind him.

<*Can we go to the place? I'm hungry.*>

<*Later. Where did the rock monster go?*>

<*In-between. It turned to come here, then turned around, then went in-between. I did not follow because you said to help the bear girl.*>

<*Good boy. You don't follow strange creatures around—rock monsters or lizards with delusions of grandeur.*>

"Your assessment, Ursula?" Monty asked when she stepped close. "What did you gather?"

"Breaking his line of sight is going to be nearly impossible," she said. "Tonight he was just testing the defenses. The golem is resilient."

"Agreed. Were you able to damage it?" Monty asked, nodding. "How effective was your hammer?"

"Between me and your extra—sized hellhound"—she rubbed Peaches' head—"we managed to slow it down. I don't think we can stop it entirely. I knocked car—sized chunks off of it, only to have them reassemble into the golem. Even Peaches' laser eye beams only punched temporary holes in it."

"I see," Monty said. "We will need to take measures."

"No kidding," I said. "Maybe we need the entire Council on this one."

"They won't be of assistance," Monty said, and Ursula shook her head. "Not this or any time, I'm afraid. At least, not until your vampire is back in control."

"What are you talking about?" I asked. "I'll call Ken. I'm sure he'll agree to give us a hand. The city is in danger, they'll have to help."

"Feel free," Monty said. "I don't think you will enjoy

the outcome, but don't let me stop you. By all means, please give them a call."

I pulled out my phone and dialed Ken.

"Strong," Ken's clipped voice answered when the call connected. "Where's my sister?"

"The last time I saw her, we were in Japan."

"I know that," he answered. "I meant after you met. Why isn't she back here? You're back, but she isn't."

"Have you met your sister? No one tells her what to do or when."

I heard a string of Japanese words and realized he was cursing. It was surprising that curses sounded like curses in almost every language.

"Why are you calling me?" Ken asked. "I'm trying to keep the Council from imploding—in case you were wondering. I'm a little busy."

"I'm calling because we have a situation."

"*You* have a situation, not *we*."

"This concerns the city, Ken. Get your head out of your—"

"You don't get it, Strong," Ken said, cutting me off. "You and your agency aren't part of the Council. We owe you no allegiance. You don't work for us, and we don't work for you."

"This situation concerns the city—the one you live in. We may not work for each other, but—"

"Our goals may have aligned in the past. That ended when your mage tried to destroy the city with Hades. If you have a situation, it didn't start because of the Dark Council, which means you can solve it without our assistance."

"Are you being serious right now?"

"Like a sword to the heart, Strong," Ken said. "You've only been alive this long because Michiko cares for you. Right now, that's the only thing holding back a full-out attack on you and your agency. They fear her—more than they hate you."

"Well, fuck you very much, Ken. You and the Dark Council."

"I can't help you, Strong. The Dark Council has unofficially put you and your people on the KOS list. Do you know what that is?"

"Yes," I said, surprised, but not really. "Kill on sight."

"Good, then I don't have to explain it to you. I shouldn't even be taking your call. You have some extremely angry Council members who want you dead, repeatedly. Starting with the Weres in the DCE."

I didn't bother trying to explain what happened or how there were extenuating circumstances. The bottom line was that we had been headed in this direction for a while now. I just hoped I didn't have to face Ken on a dark street one night. Only one of us would be walking away from that meeting.

"Thanks for the heads up, Ken," I said, and meant it. "You've always been solid."

"Listen," he said, his voice softening slightly. "You want to help your cause and keep the Council in check? Find my sister and get her back here. Until that happens—watch your six."

He ended the call.

TWENTY-SEVEN

"Kill on sight," I said as we headed back to the Command Vehicle. "After all the times we helped them?"

"No, after all the times we helped your vampire," Monty said. "Don't conflate the two. There are factions within the Council that don't like you."

"Don't...like...me?" I asked, incredulously. "What are you talking about?"

"One second," Monty said, raising a finger. "Ursula, where is the strongest hub in the network?"

"That would have to be NP-11. It's the central hub where several points overlap. That would be a beast to take, though. It's incredibly fortified."

"Where is it?" Monty asked. "In order to be an appealing target, it would need an immense amount of energy."

"It's one of the most visited places in the city and gets nearly one hundred thousand people every New Year's Eve," Ursula said. "The hub underneath Times is entered by the police station right in the center of the Square."

"Times Square? I thought that number was closer to one million?"

"Not unless each of those people were only an inch high. They aren't getting near one million—don't believe the hype."

"You need to inform your people and fortify that position," Monty said. "That will be Toson's next target."

"Only if he wants to die," Ursula said. "He tries to take that hub, he unleashes all of the city's defenses. They will come down on him so damn hard his head will spin."

"Tell me again how you stopped the golem tonight?" Monty asked. "How would you rate the effectiveness of your deterrence?"

"Well, damn. Not effective at all."

"That was with you, as a null, unleashing your power. The golem is a siphon. What do you think will happen when the city's 'defenses' are unleashed? Those who aren't nulls will—?"

"Feed that thing," Ursula said. "This is not good."

"Not in the least," Monty agreed. "Please have your people prepare as many fortifications as possible."

"I'll get right on it," Ursula said. "Do you have a timetable?"

"I placed a limiter on the artifact he's using to control the golem," Monty said, rubbing his chin. "It will take him a few days to unravel it. Three days. By then, he will be ready to move against the central hub. You have that long to shore up the defenses."

"That's not much time. How do you know he won't try to attack before then?"

"Because Toson isn't strong enough to do this without

the golem. He's counting on the city sending defenses to feed the creature—"

"Which will siphon the mages," I said. "Transferring the energy to Toson and increasing his power."

"If he's only a shift or two away from Archmage..." Monty began.

"That energy boost will push him over the edge," I finished. "He'd be an Archmage plus. A Super Saiyan Archmage—that would be bad."

"Yeah, sure," Ursula said, looking at me strangely. "I'd better go see to those defenses. I'll keep in touch."

She left us and headed to the far end of the cordon, where she jumped into a black 1947 Plymouth Business Coupe. The car was covered in the strangest runes I'd ever seen, besides the Dark Goat.

"That is one sweet ride," I said as she sped away with a roar and a rumble. "You think that's a SuNaTran vehicle?"

"Without question, considering her line of work."

"What did you mean when you said the Dark Council didn't like me?" I asked. "Not that I need them to, mind you."

"You are the living embodiment of everything they have lost, while maintaining some semblance of normalcy," Monty said. "You have the best of both worlds while belonging to neither."

"What?"

"They have lost their humanity, which many long for, while gaining abilities and longevity of life," Monty explained. "You have retained the semblance of humanity and have attained immortality, while gaining abilities. It stands to reason they would dislike you."

"But like you said, I don't belong to either of those worlds. I'm not entirely human nor entirely supernatural."

"I'd argue you are more supernatural than normal, based on the premise of immortality alone, but this is your dilemma to reconcile, not mine. We each have our burdens to carry. Some heavier than others."

We arrived at the Command Vehicle as Ramirez stepped out.

"Did you kill it?" Ramirez asked, expectantly. "Is the stone thing gone?"

"Not yet," I said. "How many people do you have in the NYTF, and how possible would it be to close down Times Square?"

"Close down Times Square?" Ramirez asked, and then broke out in laughter. It died down suddenly when we didn't join him. "You're serious?"

"Yes. We think the next attack will be in Times."

"You think? I can't make a request to shut down the busiest intersection in the city on an 'I think.' I need to be certain, and even then, no guarantees."

"The most powerful hub in the city is located in Times Square," Monty said. "We have three days to prepare the area and devise a method to stop the mage controlling the golem."

"Three days?" Ramirez asked. "That's insane. Can't be done."

"If we fail," Monty continued, "he will become even stronger and wipe us out. Do you want to take a chance on making that call, or wait to see if we were right as we die fighting for our lives?"

"Make the call, Angel," I said. "If we're wrong, we'll take the heat. If we're right, you get the glory."

"If you're wrong, my time in the NYTF will be done."

"We're not wrong. Make the call."

"What the hell," Ramirez said, after searching our faces. "Maybe it's time for an early retirement. We don't have enough NYTF to close the entire area. I'm going to have to pull personnel from other agencies."

"Get as many sensitives as you can," Monty said. "Relegate those to the inner areas. Keep the normals to the fringe areas where they will be safer."

"I really hope you aren't wrong, Strong. Now, get out of my face—I have to go put my career in jeopardy based on your hunch."

TWENTY-EIGHT

Monty had opened the cavern that passed as a trunk on the Dark Goat and retrieved another black Zegna jacket, woven with dragonscale and runed against damage. He slammed the trunk and jumped in the passenger side as I turned on the engine.

"I really hope we aren't wrong," I said as we sped uptown in the Dark Goat. "You're certain it will be in three days?"

"Not entirely," Monty answered. "There are variables."

I nearly swerved into oncoming traffic.

"What? Angel is risking everything on our recommendation. What do you mean, not entirely?"

"It was my best assessment based on the variables. The strength of the limiter I placed, factored against how proficient I thought Toson would be unraveling its design, factored against the inherent power of the Earth's Breath."

I let out a long breath. "This is bad."

"If it's any consolation," Monty said, "if I'm wrong, we

won't be around. Well maybe you'll be, but the rest of us will be killed. Toson will have become that powerful."

I glanced at him sideways as I dodged traffic.

"That...is no consolation at all. Thanks. You've been hanging around Ezra too long."

"Speaking of which, we need to go see him," Monty said. "There was something Toson said that points to someone not being entirely forthright with us."

"Ezra's always been straight with us, I mean, he's Death. Why would he lie? Besides, what would he lie about?"

"I wasn't referring to Ezra. If there is one thing I've learned in my short life, it's that, in the end, death is honest," Monty said, looking back to some far away memory. "No, I was referring to Orahjene."

"Jen? Miss 'I need to kick your ass so you can go on a suicide mission for me' Jen?" I asked. "That I can see. Do you want to call ahead? My guess is she's still in the secret garden, mid-shift."

"Good point," Monty said, pulling out his phone and connecting it to the Dark Goat. "I'd like a reservation for three, with Ezra."

"Is this an immediate reservation?" a voice asked. "Or would you like it for a later date?"

"Immediate, please. Twenty minutes."

"I have you scheduled for twenty minutes from now."

"Thank you."

He ended the call.

"Reservation for three?" I asked. "Who are you inviting?"

"You plan on leaving your creature outside?"

"Of course not," I said, glancing in the rear-view mirror

at Sir Sprawly McSprawl taking up the backseat. "I just assumed...I mean, he always goes where I go. We're bondmates."

"He still needs a reservation where we're going."

<Are we going to the place?>

<Not really, but I think I can score you extra meat for fighting the rock monster with the bear girl.>

<You are my favorite bondmate.>

<I'm your only bondmate.>

<That's why you're my favorite.>

<Flattery will get you nowhere.>

<Frank says flattery will get you everywhere. He says I should roll you up in butter to get extra meat.>

<He means butter me up, not roll me in butter.>

<Would you like that? Being rolled in butter? Will that get me extra meat?>

<You need to stop listening to that lizard.>

"I'm thinking back to what Toson said. He said too much has happened, that he can never go back. Then he mentioned Jen and something about them having a life together. Is it possible she's setting him up?"

"She could have had it all—with me," Monty said. "Those were his exact words. It speaks to a relationship of some kind."

"Yes," I said with a nod. "Sorry, my memory is a little hazy, I was a little occupied trying not to die."

"Did she want you to kill Toson to get the artifact back?"

"Funny you should ask," I said. "I asked her if she wanted him eliminated, considering he was such a threat to her and Red Mountain."

"What was her response?"

"Not if it can be avoided. She only wanted to get the Earth's Breath back."

"There is definitely more here than she shared."

"We're about to find out," I said, pulling up to the front of Ezra's deli.

We stepped out and approached the entrance. The runes on the threshold pulsed violet as we opened the door—and stepped into the secret garden.

"Extraordinary," Monty said, looking behind us. "Trans-dimensional portal physics without an external apparatus. Fascinating."

"You can go full Vulcan another time," I snapped, looking around for Ezra. "Where is he?"

"I don't think you're here to see him, are you?" Jen said from the bench. "You want to speak to me, about Toson."

"You're right," I said. "We had an interesting conversation with him. Who is he—to you specifically?"

"Toson...is my husband.

"Your what?" I said in disbelief. "Come again?"

"He was my love," Jen said, staring unflinchingly into my eyes, "and is my sworn enemy."

TWENTY-NINE

"I'm out," I said, throwing my hands in the air. "Did you hear her? Toson is her husband...No, I want no part of this. I told you, Monty, I told you: Help me, Obi Wan—"

"Simon, calm down," Monty said, raising a hand. "We haven't heard the whole—"

"Calm down?" I asked, raising my voice. "He's...her... husband. *Husband,* Monty. Why should I be calm? We don't do marriage counseling, and let me tell you"—I pointed at Jen—"you two need some serious therapy. Toson wants to kill you."

"I know," Jen answered. "I'm afraid his feeling aren't without some merit. I stopped his takeover of the Red Mountain."

"Explain," Monty said, crossing his arms and giving me a look that said, *Hear her out, then decide.* "What happened?"

I pulled out my flask and took a swig, because if there was ever a time I needed to drink something potent—this was it. I took a deep breath and exhaled...slowly. The Javambrosia coursed through my veins and immediately filled me with divine coffee goodness. I was still livid, but at least I had my coffee. Everything was manageable with a strong cup of coffee.

"Yes, please explain," I said. "Explain to us how you conveniently omitted the little detail that the mage you wanted us to face was your very pissed-off psycho husband."

"Simon…" Monty started.

"No, Tristan," Jen said, raising a hand. "He's right. I should have told you the truth from the beginning."

"Why didn't you?" Monty asked. "Despite Simon's reaction, he can actually be quite reasonable on rare occasions."

"Gee, thanks," I said, glaring at Monty. "It's not that you're married,—that's irrelevant— it's that you used us as your blunt instrument. You knowingly put our lives in jeopardy, without giving us the opportunity to choose if we wanted to be in that situation. By robbing us of the choice, you played god. You have no idea how I detest gods and their games—and you…you played us. I'm fucking done."

I walked off and left her alone with Monty. I headed into the small grove of trees with my hellhound by my side.

"That was pretty self-righteous of you," Ezra said, appearing next to me. "You sure told her."

"Are you saying I'm wrong?"

"One second," Ezra said, pointing to the ground and summoning an enormous titanium bowl filled with pastrami. "There you go. I know you've been a good boy."

Peaches looked at me and then back at the bowl, barely containing himself. If he vibrated any faster, he'd shake himself out of the plane.

<Go ahead. Don't forget to say 'thank you'. Nicely.>
<Meat is life!>

Peaches padded up to Ezra and nudged him in the leg —hard. Ezra barely moved and chuckled, patting Peaches on the head.

"You're welcome. Please wait here, Peaches," Ezra said, then pointed at me. "Walk with me."

"Sure," I said, looking around. "It's not like I have somewhere to go in this place."

A path appeared beside us, leading into a thicker part of the grove.

"You feel betrayed."

"Ezra, I'm not a prima donna," I answered. "I've done some dark shit in my life. Things I'm not proud of. Things that haunt me to this day."

"I know," Ezra answered. "I was there."

"Yes...yes you were. This is about the principle of the thing. She used us...used me. It's like these gods and their stupid, lethal, ego-games. Where we're just the unknowing pawns."

"What is the principle you're arguing? Please share."

"You want me to go after someone, don't play the victim. Own your shit, and be straight from the beginning. I'd respect that more than 'Oh, I should've told you—I'm sorry'."

"Yet, you didn't ask her pertinent questions."

"Excuse me?"

"You didn't ask *why* she wanted Toson spared, if possible," Ezra answered. "That didn't seem important?"

"Of course, it's important. I was just focused on not getting slammed during the...examination," I said when the realization hit me. "The motive. Finding the motive was part of the examination?"

"There are always layers when you learn to see," Ezra said with a nod. "Do you love Michiko?"

"Ezra, what the—? What does that have to do with this?"

"It's a simple question, isn't it?"

"Yes...no. Not really. It's complicated."

"Only if you make it so."

"I still don't see what that has to do with—?"

"Orahjene found the love of her life in the Red Mountain, many ages ago. They shared centuries together...until he wanted more."

"More? More what?"

"More recognition, more power," Ezra said with a shrug. "He was no longer content with living a life of love with his wife, Orahjene, so he devised a scheme."

"The Earth's Breath."

"Yes. You see, Orahjene was, and still is, next in line to become the First Elder. As her husband, Toson would have shared in the duties with her—together. That wasn't enough; his pride wouldn't allow him to accept those conditions."

"He stole the Earth's Breath?"

"Not only stole," Ezra answered as we passed the tranquil scene of the grove. I noticed the gentle breeze snaking its way through the leaves and branches. "Like you and your blade, the Earth's Breath was bonded to a keeper. In order for Toson to steal it—"

"He had to kill the keeper."

"He could have stopped there, but he went a step further. In his quest for power, he used the Earth's Breath to create the golem and fed the keeper's energy signature to the Earth's Breath to do so."

"Who was the keeper?"

"That keeper was the previous First Elder—and Orahjene's father," Ezra said, before pausing.

"That golem has the essence of Jen's father?"

"Yes."

"Is he...is he aware of what happened to him?" I asked. "Is he still in the golem somewhere?"

"No, the golem is not sentient. It uses the essence as fuel. The golem is not Orahjene's father, but his essence was used in creating it."

We walked on in silence as I tried to process what Jen was going through.

"Why does she want to save him?"

"Does she?" Ezra asked. "What gives you that impression?"

"She asked me not to kill him if possible, and to only bring back the Earth's Breath," I said. "Maybe she has other plans?"

"According to the Red Mountain sect, the First Elder must uphold and enforce the law in the instance of a crime," Ezra said. "That is the role of the First Elder. They serve as what you would know as a Chief Justice."

"What does their law say in this case?" I asked, hoping it would be life without parole. "He gets put away forever?"

"Not in this case. Under Red Mountain law, due to the nature of this crime, it's a life for a life."

"That's why she wanted him apprehended if possible. If someone else caught him, someone who wasn't part of the Red Mountain—?"

"She is trying to create a loophole where there isn't one —the law is clear. If she doesn't carry out this decree, the other Elders of the Red Mountain will be forced to act, declaring her in dereliction of her duty."

"I know what that means," I said, remembering the Magistrates after Monty. "Magistrates?"

Ezra shook his head.

"Nothing so nice," he said, wagging a finger. "Executioners. Remember, this isn't the casting of a forbidden rune in a populated city. This is taking a life."

"But she's mid-shift," I said. "She can't face him."

"Her shift will end in three days, and then she will be a true First Elder," Ezra answered. "Whether she chooses to stop him is another matter. We make our choices and live or die with the consequences."

"What happens if she doesn't fulfill her duty?"

"She will be stripped of her title and accepts the judgement."

"Which is?"

"I explained that already, Simon," Ezra said, gently. "A life for a life."

THIRTY

We had wound through the grove and ended up back at the bench with Jen and Monty.

Monty gave me a short glare that said, *I understand your anger, but you are still acting like a child*. I returned a glare that said *I know you are, but what am I?*, at which, he rolled his eyes and sighed.

"I understand if you no longer wish to help me," Jen said. "What I did was deceptive, and I make no excuses for my behavior."

"I'll help you," I said. "But only if you're honest with me. Are you planning on going after him?"

"I plan on saving him," she answered, "to the best of my ability."

"What if he can't be saved? What if he's too far gone?"

"Then I will uphold the law."

"Fuck," I said. "What if Monty and I stop him? What happens if we apprehend him?"

Jen smiled and shook her head.

"There is an obscure statute that states if a criminal is apprehended by someone other than a member of our sect, then that judgment rests in the hands of the apprehending party. Clemency can be petitioned to the Elder of the sect."

"Then we do that," I said. "Monty and I will catch him. We can petition clemency, and they can lock him up instead of killing him."

"He's too powerful," Jen said. "I can't ask this of you."

"You're not asking. We've already accepted," I said. "Plus, there's that whole matter of his wanting to attack my city again."

"There is that," Monty said. "We can't let him access that hub or form his golem army."

"I would be eternally in your debt if you stopped him," Jen said. "I have three more days left to my shift."

"Three days?" Monty asked, narrowing his eyes slightly. "Are you certain?"

"Quite," Jen said with a tight smile. "I think I'm quite capable of judging the duration of my shift, thank you. I happen to be several centuries your senior, Tristan."

"Forgive my impudence," Monty said with a slight bow. "I meant no disrespect."

"Only if you forgive my outburst."

"Think nothing of it," Monty said, glancing at me. "Please continue—your shift in three days?"

"Of course," Jen said. "Once it's complete, you must allow me to assist you in this matter. It's the least I can do. It is my duty."

"Tell you what," I said, raising a hand. "You worry about getting through your shift. Monty and I will worry about stopping Toson. We'll let you know where we are when we stop him—fair?"

"More than. Please be careful."

We walked to the edge of the grove, following Ezra.

"Can we get a non-agonizing port back to our place?" I asked. "Please?"

Ezra chuckled, and then grew serious. "The non-agonizing part depends on you," he said. "Measure your words carefully today. You have set things in motion, and not everything is as it seems."

"Welcome to my life," I said. "Thanks for the talk, Ezra."

"I should be thanking you. Be careful with Toson and the golem. Do not take either of them lightly."

He waved a hand, and the secret garden vanished from sight.

When I could see again, we were in our apartment.

"Do you think he moves the Dark Goat, too, when he pulls off these super ports?" I asked. "Can you do that?"

"I think he doesn't forget details like our transportation. I think Uncle Dex would be the closest to Ezra in teleportational skill. I still have much to learn."

"I don't trust her, Monty. I told her to be honest and she tried to BS me."

"What do you mean?" Monty said, heading to the kitchen. "I really need a cuppa."

"Ezra said she tried to find a loophole where there wasn't one, for starters. All of a sudden there's an obscure statute? Please, sell that to someone else. She wants to dust Toson."

"Is it possible that she knows more about Red Mountain legalities than, say, someone who has no clue about their laws—like you?"

"She said he *was* her love, but *is* her sworn enemy. Words matter. The rage is right there, seething under the surface—trust me. I know the feeling of rage. The smell is familiar."

"According to Orahjene, Toson *killed* her father, fed his essence to the Earth's Breath and created a golem," Monty said. "I could see her harboring some animosity toward her husband or anyone who took those actions."

"True, I'd want to dust him based on that myself," I said, rubbing my chin. "Something still feels off."

"Quite. There is the small matter that her shift is complete, and she tried to mask it—quite effectively, I might add. If I were a less experienced mage, I would have missed it."

"Her shift is complete?" I asked. "Then what is she doing? Waiting for us to flush out Toson?"

"Most likely," Monty replied. "I highly doubt she will sacrifice herself for him. He betrayed her and killed her family. An offense under their law—punishable by death."

"She's going to wait until he makes his move, intercept him, and put him down?" I asked. "Do you think Ezra knows?"

Monty nodded.

"It's not Ezra's place to pass judgment. In the grand scheme of things, he is the answer to everything."

"Well, that's not morbid or anything, Darth Montague."

"Orahjene is angry and wants revenge," Monty said matter-of-factly. "She may have loved Toson, once, but that love is gone now, leaving only hatred in its wake. Like you said earlier—the rage is right there, seething under the surface."

"My intuition tells me she's going to try and end it all," I said, pointing at him. "I think she's going for the nuclear option—take Toson, herself, and anyone unlucky enough to be at ground zero."

"That would be our city," Monty said, "and us."

"Some people just want to see the world burn. She may still love him, but can't bring herself to forgive him."

"Then it's not love, Simon."

"Regardless, I say we stop Toson and give him to the other Elders. Then we can do this clemency thing."

"What if he doesn't *want* clemency?" Monty asked. "Maybe he wants to end it all as well?"

"Well, then it all goes to shit, doesn't it? I told you this whole case was a disaster. No...you had to fall for the 'Obi Wan' line."

"For the record," Monty said, sipping his tea, "*we* fell for the Obi Wan line, you more than I, since you are the Star Warriors fan."

"Did you just say 'Star Warriors'?" I asked, insulted. "It's *Star Wars*...not Star Warriors. You don't see me calling your low-budget TV show 'Space Trek', do you?"

"Only because you know better than to mistake an insightful, intelligently written, and ground-breaking example of entertainment," he answered with a huff. "What ground did your Star Wars break? Oh, yes, I recall now...toy sales."

"You said that wrong," I countered. "Totally off."

"I beg your pardon? Which part?"

"All of it," I said, hunching my shoulders in my best Shatner. "I think what you meant to say was: I, know, better, thantomistake, a, groundbreaking, example, of, entertainment."

He stared at me and sipped his tea in silence for a few seconds.

"It's clear we need to visit Roxanne at Haven. You have most definitely suffered head trauma. How many stones hit your head?"

"Don't, you, think—?"

"I think," Monty said, cutting me off mid-Shatner, "that right now we need to focus on why Cecelia's shortcut failed to work. I thought it was sound."

"Don't tell me you're going to blame little Cece for it not working? Whatever happened to 'The teacher only shows what's needed, not everything he knows'? Maybe a certain teacher needs to hit the books a little harder?"

"Of course not," Monty answered. "Any failing on her part is directly attributed to my teaching."

"Wow, I'm impressed."

"Although, I do have to factor in for negative influences in her environment, like ill-mannered hellhounds and their bondmates, along with deluded lizards who believe they are dragons."

"Really...you're going to go there?"

"These influences are a clear and present danger to my apprentice's learning."

"You keep that up, and Cece is going to need to find a new teacher."

Monty's phone rang.

He put it on speakerphone.

"Hello? Tristan?"

"Ursula?" Monty asked, looking puzzled. "What's wrong?"

"It's better if I show you. Meet me at NP-1, now."

"What's wrong?"

"We have a major catastrophe in the making."

She ended the call.

THIRTY-ONE

"Ursula doesn't seem like the nervous type."

"That's because she isn't. If she says it's a catastrophe, rest assured, that's a conservative estimate of the situation."

"You know what I'd really like?" I asked as we sped downtown and the sun peeked over the horizon. "Just once?"

"Copious amounts of Deathwish coffee? Preferably delivered through an IV drip?"

"That's not a bad idea, but then I couldn't move around," I said, giving it some thought. "No, I'd like to get a call saying 'Hey, no need to worry, the city isn't on the verge of obliteration today.' Just once. You know?"

"I think that's being overly optimistic. The world you exist in now is not a world of rainbows and unicorns. It's a dark, dangerous, and lethal place ready to impale you with death at any moment."

"Whoa, dial back the dark side a bit there, Darth Monty," I said, glancing at him. "I know the things we do and face are dangerous, but seriously? A dark, dangerous, and lethal place ready to impale you with death?"

"Too much?" Monty asked. "It does sound a bit oppressive."

"You think?"

"I didn't finish my cuppa," he said, looking out of the window. "I can't be held responsible for my words until I've had some proper tea—with my digestives."

"Fine, I'll make sure to get you your cookies."

"They're not 'cookies,' and your 'hellhound ate them' excuse was a load of rubbish."

"Wow, you *are* cranky today. I'll get you two boxes of digestion cookies. I'll even throw in some lettuce for roughage since you need digestive help. Happy?"

"I just can't make heads or tails out of the shortcut failing."

We arrived at the Bowling Green hub with little traffic. Ursula's vehicle was parked outside, the black sheen reflecting the early morning sun. I tried to read the runes on the surface of her vehicle, but came up empty. They kept shifting and changing as I looked at them.

"What do those runes say?" I asked as we passed her car. "The symbols keep shifting around."

"Wait a second," Monty said, stopping mid-stride, snapping a finger, and turning back to examine Ursula's car. "That's it—that's what I've been missing in the short-cut. Permutational persistence!"

Monty moved to place his hand on the surface of Ursula's car.

"Do not touch the Widow," Ursula said. "She doesn't like strangers, and I don't like smudges."

"Permutational what, now?" I asked as we followed

Ursula back to the hub. Sprawly McPeaches was still snoring in the back of the Dark Goat. I thought that hitting XL, tangling with the golem, and then overstuffing himself with Ezra's pastrami was taking its toll on him. He was actually tired.

"I'll explain later," Monty said as we entered the hub. He turned and focused on Ursula. "Now, what is this catastrophe you were mentioning?"

We approached a small, nondescript building in the center of Bowling Green. It was basically a plain, small, rectangular structure about twenty feet square, on the outside. Inside, it was considerably larger, and I figured it sat sideways, somewhere adjacent to our plane, taking up more space somewhere else.

"This building is called an Oracle, and it houses a nexus point," Ursula said, pointing. "In this case, a nexus hub. One of several."

In the center of the Oracle rested a confluence of energy with extensions running in different directions. It basically looked like an active orb of violet energy with extensions shooting out from its center.

Nothing appeared to be happening.

"So, you called us down here to see your orb of energy? Where is the—?"

The orb in the center of the Oracle blasted a beam of energy straight up into the top of the structure.

"That—is not supposed to happen," Ursula said, her voice grim. "These pulses have been regular, every five minutes, since they began."

"Maybe it's bleeding off excess energy?" I suggested. "You know, clearing the energy plumbing?"

Both Monty and Ursula stared at me.

"When did they begin?" Monty asked, ignoring me and narrowing his eyes, examining the orb in the center of the building. "Do you know where they are going?"

"We calculated that they started around the time Simon fought Toson," Ursula said, looking up into the ceiling. "As for where they're going—look again. They aren't going anywhere."

I looked up when the next pulse blasted into the ceiling.

"What do you mean 'they aren't going anywhere'?" I asked. "I just saw it go up into the—"

"Bloody hell," Monty said, his voice laced with fear and anger. "That was the purpose of the attack. It wasn't a scouting mission."

"What?" I said, still not seeing it. "What did he do?"

"Look," Monty said, pointing to the ceiling. "Really look."

I did my best Eastwood-Monty impression and narrowed my eyes at the ceiling. For a few seconds, all I saw was the smooth surface of the ceiling, and then slowly, like seeing something out of the corner of your eye, figures formed—two human sized golems. Floating in space above our heads.

Another pulse blasted, and a stream of violet energy channeled into each of the golem bodies, bathing them in the energy until it was absorbed completely.

"What the fu—?" I started.

"Toson must be using the energy of the hub to feed them," Monty said, letting his gaze trace the blast of the last pulse back to the confluence. "Is it possible to shut down this hub completely?"

"Too dangerous," Ursula said. "We have line regulators

which allow the regular nexus points to be isolated if they became corrupted or fall under attack."

"We need to shut this hub down," I said, pointing up. "Toson is creating more golems up there."

"It's not that simple," Ursula said. "Every nexus point is interconnected. The hubs are unique; they hold up the framework."

"This is a poor design. Each nexus point should be able to be shut off independently."

"I'll be sure to pass on your design feedback to the originators of the nexus network," Ursula snapped. "I'm sure they'll be eager to hear your ideas."

"Can you contact them? Maybe they know a way to shut this thing down?"

"Is he always like this?" Ursula asked.

"Only when awake," Monty answered, still looking up. "You get used to it. She can't contact the original designers, Simon. This network was established a millennia ago. They're all dead by now."

"You must have incredible patience," Ursula added. "Anyway, I tried to find everything and anything on this situation. Nothing about a siphon attaching itself to a hub."

"We can't shut this down, then," I said. "It's too dangerous."

"Exactly—this is a hub with some strange siphon casting happening. I don't know what will happen if we try isolating it. It could isolate the hub, activate those golems, or just explode, and then the city will end at Canal Street."

"These points contain that much power?"

"More," Ursula answered. "If it sets off a chain reaction

throughout the network...New York will be known as the city with four boroughs."

"Three, really," I corrected. "No self-respecting New Yorker thinks Staten Island is part of the city."

"True," Ursula admitted. "I'm going to have to stay here and try to bleed the energy off the line with my hammer. This means—"

"You won't be able to face Toson at Times Square," Monty said, putting it together. "Toson is either very clever or extremely desperate."

"I'd rather deal with very clever," I said. "Clever people take steps to not make mistakes and fail. Desperate people usually accept failure as an acceptable outcome."

"Or a combination of both," Ursula added. "Maybe he knows he's cornered or running out of time, and this is a Hail Mary play."

"The orbs he fired," I said. "What if he knew Jen was close to the end of her shift? He mentioned it when we fought. He fires the orbs and starts the clock on these golems. You saw how hard it was to stop one golem. Can you imagine what he'll be like—with three?"

"I have my team looking for a way to interrupt this process," Ursula said. "In the meantime, I'd suggest you find a way to combat these things. One that doesn't require the equivalent of a runic nuke."

"I have an idea," Monty said, and I groaned inwardly. "It may be risky, but I think it can work."

"Does it involve permutational peristalsis?" I asked. "I only ask because you sound overly excited, which is usually a bad sign."

"It's permutational persistence, and rubbish, I don't sound overly excited."

"Sure, you don't."

"What does he want to do?" Ursula asked, looking at me, then at Monty. "You do sound a little on edge there, Tristan."

"This hub is a power source, correct?"

"Yes...a considerable power source," Ursula answered, clearly still unsure of where Monty was going. "One that shouldn't be tampered with—if you know what I mean?"

"It's almost identical to the Earth's Breath in design," Monty said, gesticulating. Something he did when he encountered a new theory or the possibility of blowing up the city. "I have a way to shortcut the energy output so that the energy being shunted to the golems is stopped."

"How exactly?" Ursula said, stepping in between Monty and the hub. "What is this shortcut?"

"Using permutational persistence in runes, instead of numbers, I can, in essence, 'confuse' the hub into constantly redirecting its energy through these conduits instead of into the golems above."

"Have you tried this before?" Ursula asked, and I braced myself. "Has this permutational persistence worked anywhere else?"

"This would be my first attempt," Monty admitted. "But I know it will work."

"Get out of my hub," Ursula said, forming her hammer with a crack of lightning. "Don't make me tell you again."

THIRTY-TWO

"I'd say that went rather well," Monty said when we got into the Dark Goat, and I pulled away from the near-hammering at the hands of Ursula. "Don't you think?"

"Oh, sure," I said, nodding. "Getting flattened by an angry werebear wielding a hammer of devastation is how I like to unwind, you know—take a load off. Maybe an arm or leg, too."

"I know my permutational persistence sequence can work, I just need a large enough stable power source to test it on."

"Tell me you aren't thinking what I think you're thinking."

"We need to flush out Toson."

"Agreed," I said. "How about we just give him a call? You know, something friendly and non-threatening, like: 'Hey, Toson, come out so we can shred you'?"

"This would be the equivalent of giving him the most urgent call. Without the central hub, his plan falls apart. If I can make it appear like the main hub is losing power—"

"Ursula and her team will ride in, slamming you upside the head with her hammer?" I asked. "Is that the outcome you're looking for?"

"No, Toson will come to us," Monty said. "He will think the hub has siphoned too much energy from downtown and come to investigate the central hub."

"He won't come alone—he has a golem with him," I said. "With two in the oven downtown."

"We won't allow him to activate the other two."

"Who's going to be there to stop him?"

"We'll be there to stop him," Monty countered. "The shortcut should nullify the effects of the golem's siphon."

"We didn't do so hot last time—well, you did, but I don't think that was the plan, Human Torch."

"What do you think is going to happen tonight?" Monty asked. "Once Toson knows Orahjene completed her shift?"

"He's under time pressure," I said. "He'll try to take the central hub and increase his power to match hers."

"Precisely," Monty said. "We can't let that happen."

"How strong will she be?"

"Stronger than his level right now, and clearly beyond me," Monty admitted. "This is the only window we have."

"We can't go around playing with a nexus point—not just a nexus point, the central hub," I said. "Did you forget what Ursula said about these points going off? You've never done this before."

"I find your lack of faith...disturbing."

"Did you just Vader me?"

"When have I been wrong?"

"I seem to recall facing Toson, and InvisiMonty was

nowhere to be seen because his shortcut didn't work. Does that count?"

"I wasn't wrong," he said. "I was missing information. My permutational persistence sequence is correct. I can make it work."

"I wish we had something stronger than your permutational persisting theory," I said. "Something that could solve this without all the agony and pain I sense coming our way."

"Life is pain," Monty said. "Besides, contrary to popular belief, a runic nuke does not exist."

"A runic nuke sounds like a good idea right now," I said. "Or at least one that wipes out magic. That way—"

"Don't," Monty said, his voice slicing through the Dark Goat. Even Peaches' ears perked up at his tone. "Don't ever make that suggestion in the presence of a mage or any magic-user."

"What?" I asked. "All I was suggesting, is that we use something that removes magic from the equa—"

"Simon," Monty said with a sigh. "That...is how the Supernatural War started: with those ideas. Normals felt it was better to remove magic from the equation, that life would be easier or better. The outcome of those thoughts and of the war, were horrific. The cost in life, on both sides, immeasurable."

"I understand."

"Not really, you don't—but you will. Please watch your words in the future. Some of the older mages would have taken offense. Violent offense."

"Duly noted," I said. "What are we going to do about the new golems and Toson?"

"Call Ramirez," Monty said. "Tell him we need Times Square shut down tonight."

"Are you insane? Tonight? There's no way he can pull that off."

"He can, if he uses just the NYTF."

"He doesn't have the manpower. We're being hasty. Think this through, Monty."

"We don't need all of Times Square shut down, just the center, near the station."

"Just the center? Are you listening to yourself?"

"Orahjene wants revenge," Monty said. "Toson wants power. I say we give them to each other."

"What the hell are you talking about? Did you get hit by a stone during my fight with Toson?" I asked. "Or maybe he fried some of those brain cells when he tried to barbecue you?"

"Call Ramirez," Monty said, his voice certain. "I'll make the other arrangements. We end this tonight."

THIRTY-THREE

"Are you sure about this?" I asked again before connecting the call. "Ramirez is going to go ballistic."

"I'm willing to risk the Director's ire if it means saving the city," Monty answered, his jaw set. "I've made calls to the five movie production companies. They will start bringing in the trailers and trucks around six."

"That should block the Square, but not for long," I said. "This permutation thing. How long before it takes effect?"

"The effect is immediate. Once we interrupt the flow of energy, I anticipate Toson will appear shortly after. He will think the tampering was done by Orahjene."

"...who will show up not too long after he gets here."

"She was being dishonest about her shift," Monty answered. "I'm sure she had her reasons for the subterfuge, but it still stands—her shift is complete. With her heightened power, she will know where he is once he surfaces."

"You know that once you tamper with the central hub,

the hammer-wielding, werebear protector of the nexus points, Ursula, will arrive too…right?"

"It will be some time before she gets here, due to her keeping the flow of energy regulated downtown. We should be done before she gets on site."

I took a long breath and let it out slowly.

"Here we go," I said, connecting the call to Ramirez. "I hope you're ready."

"Strong," Ramirez growled. "To what do I owe the displeasure?"

"Tristan wants to speak to you, Angel."

"The answer is no," Ramirez said, preemptively. "I don't know what you want, but the answer is no."

"Hear me out, Director."

"No," Ramirez said. "You can't imagine the number of favors I had to call in to get Times Square closed in three days."

"What if I told you this could be an NYTF operation only?" Monty asked. "You keep your favors uncalled for another day and we only use your people?"

"I'd say I don't have enough people to shut down Times Square."

I was noticing a distinct lack of screaming and ranting.

"You do, if a major blockbuster film will be shooting there tonight."

"We don't have a major—wait, *you* mobilized all those production companies?" Ramirez asked. "How did you get the permits?"

Monty glanced my way. "I know a gentleman who knows a gentleman."

I sighed and shook my head.

"Angel," I interrupted. "We aren't closing Times Square

for the whole night. One, maybe two hours, tops. The movie trucks and trailers will be the outer cordon keeping out pedestrians. NYTF and EMTe will form the inner cordon around the police station. What do you think?"

Asking Ramirez his opinion wasn't going to change the outcome of Monty's actions tonight. I knew Monty well enough to know he had entered his "hurricane track" of execution. His plan was going to go through with or without NYTF cooperation—like a force of nature. It would just be easier and contain much less screaming if Ramirez was on board.

"I think you're both insane," Ramirez said, pausing for a few beats. "But it could work. How soon do I need to re-route my people to Times?"

"The trucks will arrive at six," Monty said. "By the time they set up and shut down the streets, we're looking at a few hours. The NYTF should be there half-past five to start redirecting pedestrian and vehicular traffic."

"How far out from the station do we need to control?" Ramirez asked. "More importantly, will my people be in danger?"

"The moment you see us, pull your people back at least two blocks," Monty said. "That should keep them safe. We'll control the area near the station."

"Is that rock thing showing up again tonight?"

"Yes," Monty said. "But this is New York. No one gets fazed in this city...right?"

"Got that right. You need to keep any and all damage centralized. If you two renovate Times Square, you better look for another city to call home."

"Understood," Monty and I said in unison. "See you tonight."

"We need to go prepare the area," Monty said, looking at his watch, which caught my eye. "Let's head to Times Square."

"You stopped wearing the Patek?" I asked curiously. "Since when?"

"Since an orb of energy cracked the case, followed by the movement deciding to take an extended leave of absence."

"What is that now? It looks decidedly non-Montague like. Functional and ugly."

"This is a Lemania 5100," Monty said, holding up his wrist. "It's not aesthetic, but it works and has the added bonus of being the only watch Cecil was able to rune against massive damage."

"Now, all you need—is to do the same thing to your clothes."

"Cecil refuses to rune my wardrobe," Monty said, irritated. "Said it would be a bloody waste of time and clothing."

"I'm going to go with Cecil on this one."

"Can you park near Bryant Park? We can walk from there to the central hub."

"What do you need at Bryant Park?"

"Insurance," Monty said and went silent, gazing out of the window. "The kind I hope we don't need."

THIRTY-FOUR

We arrived at Bryant Park.

I parked and locked the Dark Goat. Peaches climbed the steps to the library next to me as passersby gave us a wide berth. I wanted to imagine it was my subtle vibe of rugged danger, but it was most likely the large hellhound walking by my side, not wearing a leash.

I left the Dark Goat on Fifth Avenue in front of the New York Public Library. The lions—Patience and Fortitude, named by Mayor LaGuardia—looked down at us as we headed past the library and to the large lawn situated behind it. I had a feeling we would need both of them tonight.

"You plan on getting some leisure time in?" I asked, walking past New Yorkers lounging in the sun, enjoying a slice of nature in the center of the concrete jungle I called home. "Maybe a spot of tea on the grass before we fight for our lives tonight?"

"I don't do leisure time in the grass," Monty answered and cut right, onto the sidewalk. "This way."

<Can I go roll in the grass?>

<I'm trying to imagine a scenario where that doesn't end in a mass panic of people running for their lives, out of the park.>

<Is that a no?>

<That...is a definite no.>

<You're the one that said I needed exercise. If I roll in the grass and people run, I can chase them. That will be exercise. I won't bite them.>

<That scenario will go from mass panic to a state of emergency. We'd probably have the National Guard surrounding the park in record time to deal with you.>

<That still sounds like a no.>

<Because it is a no. Besides, you need to ease into the exercise. You seemed a little tired after your XL adventure yesterday. Are you okay?>

<I was a little tired. I think I ate too much meat.>

<Is there such a thing? I'm shocked.>

<Me, too. But I'm working to do better.>

Monty headed down a stairway on 42nd Street that seemed to lead to the subway, but actually led to a closed door. He looked behind him to make sure we were behind him.

"Stay close to me," Monty said. "If you don't enter with me, you will remain outside."

"What is this? Where does it lead?"

"This leads to the Stacks—the old magical storage beneath the park."

"Wait, I thought the Milstein Stacks were part of the library. They're for storing books."

"They are. I never said the Milstein Stacks. Those do exist for book storage. The stacks I'm referring to, the

Arcanum Obscura, are much deeper, starting at one hundred feet below the park.

"The Arcanum? Didn't you say it was sealed?" I said, looking at the plain black door. "Was it opened recently?"

"Not really," Monty answered, cryptically. "At least, not officially."

"'Not officially' sounds like we're breaking in."

"'Not officially' means it doesn't actually exist to break into," Monty said, pressing certain sections of the door. "We can't break into a place that doesn't exist, can we?"

"Right," I said as the door opened slowly inward. "This is us not breaking into a place that doesn't exist—perfect. Now, *I'm* starting to sound like Ziller."

"This way," Monty said, moving fast. "We mustn't dawdle."

"Dawdle? The last thing I want to do in this place, is dawdle," I said, looking around, dawdling. "This place is enormous."

"Yes, it is," Monty hissed. "Stay close."

The Arcanum was setup in the typical warehouse style on a massive scale. If Home Depot and Costco had a baby, they would give birth to the Arcanum. I tried looking down the corridors to see the other end, and couldn't. Huge didn't begin to describe it. This place was large enough to require its own zip code.

"Helloooo!" I yelled and waited for my echo. My voice came back to me a few seconds later. "Wow, that is immense."

"Did you forget the part where I mentioned the Arcanum is guarded?" Monty asked, grabbing my arm and pulling me out of sight and into one of the corridors off the main passageway. A large iron man, like some renegade from Fritz Lang's Metropolis, appeared a few seconds later, making absolutely no noise as it walked by.

"What is that?" I asked when the guardian had walked out of sight.

"That is an Arcanum guardian," Monty said, peeking around the corner. "Think magical null to the nth degree. No magical, and very few conventional, weapons work against those things."

"How can they still be functioning?"

"Do you really want to find out?"

"Not really," I said, realizing I'd like to exit the Arcanum as soon as possible after seeing that thing. "Are we trespassing?"

"What do you think?" Monty asked, before raising a hand and pulling out a small notebook. "Be silent and give me a second. I need to orient myself"—he looked down at his book—"locate the item, and get us out of here. I can't do that if you keep asking me questions."

"Can I ask you one more question?" I said. "I'm curious about something."

"What is it now?" Monty snapped. "I just told you I needed to focus on—"

"How fast do they move?" I asked, looking behind Monty at the tall iron man staring blankly at us. "Just asking for a friend."

Monty turned slowly and looked up at the guardian, who had frozen in place.

"Simon, stay absolutely still," Monty said, passing me his open notebook. "They track runic energy signatures. Right now, it's assessing the threat I pose. Do you see the item in my book?"

I glanced down at the book and saw a vial of dark liquid under the words *Mors Tenebris*—Dark Death.

"I see it," I said, quietly. "What is this?"

"I'll explain later," Monty answered, keeping his voice low. "I'm going to run behind you and get its attention. Wait until you can no longer see or hear me, then you need to go ten aisles left and three sections right. Did you get that?"

"Wait until you're gone. Ten aisles left, three sections right. Will I be able to see such a small vial?"

"You won't be able to miss it. It will be a small black case and feel like death has gripped you. Once you find it, use your creature to get out. You will never find the door without me. Ready?"

"Stop asking me that. I'm never ready. This is insane."

"We've done worse. Remember, wait until I'm gone before you move."

He slowly turned away from the guardian and bolted behind me.

The guardian followed silently several seconds later.

THIRTY-FIVE

<Where is the angry man going?>

<He's going to take the big metal man away from us.>

<Is he scared?>

<He's keeping us safe. We have to find a small box. Come on.>

I waited until Monty was gone from sight and moved fast. Ten aisles left, I turned right and headed down for three sections when a wave of darkness filled my thoughts.

<This place feels bad. Can we go back?>

<This is the place we need. Once we get the box we can leave.>

<This place makes my stomach feel bad, like your meat, but without the meat.>

<I know boy. Mine, too. We're almost out of here. Give me a second.>

I searched the shelves until the feeling of oppression and sadness grew stronger. There, sitting on the shelf, around eye-level, sat a small black box. Beneath it, on the shelf was a small tag that read: *Mors Tenebris*—Dark Death.

Honestly, it didn't need the tag. I took the box and grabbed Peaches by the scruff.

<Take us to the grass, boy. Now.>

The Arcanum Obscura disappeared from sight and the bright green of Bryant Park rushed up to greet my face, as I landed on the lawn as gracefully as a cinder block. Several of the people closest to me looked up from their tablets and electronics, made a mental note that I must have appeared from somewhere above, and went back to their electronics.

<Can I chase them now?>

<Do not chase anyone. You can let them pet you, but no biting.>

<It's not as fun when I can't bite.>

<Do you want meat later?>

<Yes. I'm starving again.>

<Then no biting.>

<What if they bite me first?>

<No one is going to bite you, first or second. Let's go.>

I got shakily to my feet and started heading off the lawn to the 42nd Street side. There, at the stairwell leading to the Arcanum Obscura, stood Monty. He extended a hand, and I gave him the box of death. I noticed he was banged up with facial scratches and some bruises. The rear of his jacket had a long tear down the center.

"Your jacket—" I started.

"I know," he snapped as we started heading west to Times Square.

"It's really shredded."

"I'm aware of its condition."

"Do we have a spare in the Dark Goat?"

"This is the spare from the car."

"Oh," I said, at a loss. "Those guardians really hit hard, don't they?"

"You don't say?" Monty said, shrugging off the jacket. He tore it in two and dropped the pieces in a nearby wastebasket as he stared at me. "Whatever gave you that impression?"

"What is Dark Death?" I asked. "The real answer, not the classic magespeak response."

"It accelerates a transformation into darkness," Monty said, fixing me with his gaze. "For a mage of a certain skill, it pushes the level of power into Archmage territory for a short time, if he uses blood magic."

"What happens after that 'short time' is up?"

"Don't ask questions you know the answer to," Monty snapped. "It's insulting. The outcome is in the name."

We walked in silence until we arrived at Times Square. By the time we arrived, I had grown certain of a few things. First among them—I wasn't going to lose my family. Not to a psycho pair of earth mages nor to some toxic mage accelerant. Not today...not any day.

"You can't use that thing," I said when we got to the front of the precinct. "You can't use the Dark Death."

"I told you," Monty said. "It's insurance. Better to have it and not need it, than need it and not have it."

I outstretched my hand.

"Don't make me ask again," I said, keeping my arm extended. "I'll hold it."

"You can't use it, Simon. What purpose would it serve if you held it?"

"Here's the thing about that kind of insurance," I said, my arm still out. "Somehow, someway, the occasion always comes up when it's needed. I'll hold it."

He removed the box from his pocket and looked down at it, then handed it to me. I opened the box to make sure the vial of black liquid was inside.

"Whatever you do—do *not* ingest that liquid," Monty said. "You're not a mage. I don't know what it will do to you."

"Guess that means neither of us will find out what it does today."

"You can be truly exasperating at times," Monty said, rolling up his sleeves. "I don't know why I put up with you."

"Don't you have runes to place around this area?" I asked, deflecting. "It's almost time, and you still haven't done your computational analysis."

"Yes, mother, and it's permutational persistence, get it right," he said, observing the perimeter of the Square around the police station. "Can't you remember the simplest things? You have a memory like a sieve."

"That's what I have you for, WikiMonty."

He threw a hand up in the air and started walking the perimeter. Every so often, I would see him crouch and inscribe golden symbols into the ground that glowed brightly for a few seconds before fading.

I opened the box holding the *Mors Tenebris* and removed the vial. I opened my flask, walked over to a nearby trashcan and dumped out half of the javambrosia.

I proceeded to drink the rest. I had a feeling I was going to need the jolt it provided—and besides, dumping all of it just seemed...criminal. I opened the vial and poured the contents in my flask. It refilled daily with my javambrosia, but for now it would only hold Dark Death.

I stepped over to a vending machine with Peaches in

tow and bought a Coke. I filled the vial with the soda, resealed it, and placed it in the box. An officer from the precinct stepped over to me.

"Excuse me, sir," the officer said, keeping one hand on the butt of his gun. "I'm afraid you can't have your...dog... in such a populated area without a leash."

"I understand," I said, flashing my ID, which usually resolved these issues. He wasn't impressed. "Tell you what, we're going to do a shoot this afternoon"—I looked at his name tag—"Officer Brown. How about I get you an autograph?"

"What are you filming?"

"Mission Impossible: StoneStrike," I said, improvising on the spot. "Mr. Cruise's people will be here shortly. Do you want to meet him?"

"Nah, I'm done with Cruise," Brown said. "Who's the female lead?"

"None other than the Black Widow herself, Scarlet Johansson. Maybe I can arrange a meet with her?"

"Saw her in that Marvel flick, the Revengers—end of the game, the one where she bites it—wasn't impressed."

New Yorkers—tough crowd. I opted for reverse psychology.

"Who *are* you a fan of?" I asked. "Anyone you want to meet?"

"That Matrix guy—John Kwik," Brown said, full of conviction. "Him."

"Mr. Reeves?"

"Yeah, him!" Brown said, snapping his fingers. "Is he in this one?"

"I was just about to say his name," I said with a laugh. "You must have read my mind."

"No shit, really?" Brown said with a chuckle. "You think I can get a selfie with him? Now that guy is badass. You never touch the dog."

"I agree," I said, glancing at Peaches. "He is a badass."

"Can I meet him ?"

"As soon as he gets on set, I'll have his people look for you," I said, squinting at his name tag. "Officer Brown, right?"

"That's me," he said. "I'll be just inside."

"Do I still need to—?" I asked, pointing at Peaches. "He's really well-trained."

"Look"—he looked to the side—"as long as you can keep him close to you, and maybe you stand over there, away from the precinct? That way my supervisors don't see you, know what I mean? Then it should be good."

"Got it," I said as we shook hands, and I moved off to the side. "Thanks."

I looked across the street from where I stood in front of the station. Catty-corner to where I was, I saw the Hard Rock Cafe Restaurant. On the other side of the precinct, from 43rd Street to 44th Street, the sidewalk had been converted into a broad pedestrian walkway to deal with the influx of tourists and pedestrian traffic.

The precinct itself stood sandwiched between 7th Avenue and Broadway. Ursula wasn't joking about it being fortified. I could feel the undercurrent of hub energy of the nexus point behind me. The officers in the precinct gave off a particular energy signature that delivered a subtle message—"Come try us, so we can end you"—in a concentrated dose.

Behind me and the precinct stood One Times Square, the building where the Tiffany crystal ball dropped every

December 31st, ushering in the new year. I looked at the many clocks around the Square. We had a few hours to go.

The name Times Square was deceptive. The area was known as the crossroads of the world with good reason. Everyone wanted to be here, but it wasn't exactly a square. It was shaped like a skewed hourglass where several streets intersected, creating an intersection of humanity and barely controlled chaos.

Monty circled back to the front of the precinct, saw me, and walked over to where I stood. He held an actual china cup of Earl Grey.

"Where did you get that?" I asked. "They let you walk out with the cup?"

"Apparently, I have charms," Monty said. "The barista nearly swooned when she saw me. Kept calling me Tom Middlestrom or some such. I was afraid for her safety. In any case, she prepared this excellent cuppa of Earl Grey and allowed me to walk off with the cup—free of charge."

"You are incredible," I said, shaking my head. "We aren't here to seduce baristas, you know."

"Well, the perimeter is secure," he said, after taking a sip and moaning with pleasure. "The outer perimeter will lock us in, and keep everyone out."

"What about in here?"

"Once Ramirez gets his people out, I'll activate the inner cordon. We'll contain any damage to this area. Did you get a read on how protected the central hub is?"

"Considerably," I said. "I counted at least ten officers I could see and they were alert. Do you need to get in there?"

"Without question," Monty said. "The access to the Oracle is downstairs."

"You have a plan for extricating the officers from the heavily guarded precinct?"

"I do," he answered with a smile. "It doesn't even involve anything blowing up."

"That'll be a first."

THIRTY-SIX

Turns out, some of the runes Monty knew were from his misspent youth, where he would convince some of his instructors at the Golden Circle that something had died in the classroom and was currently rotting away.

When the first production trucks started rolling in, Monty unleashed his rune of putrefaction right on the precinct. The odor that enveloped the area was nose-destroying, nearly making me gag. It smelled like a platoon of skunks had decided to launch an all-out attack on Times Square.

Surprisingly, as resilient as New Yorkers were, even they succumbed to the odor, giving the area a wide berth and keeping to the edges until asked to leave the area by production personnel.

Soon afterward, NYTF officers entered the scene and people started clearing out the area.

"What the hell died in here?" Ramirez boomed as he approached us. "Was this you, Strong? Don't you bathe?"

"Do you think you could clear out the precinct for us?"

Monty asked. "I need to reach the lower level to get the events of the evening started."

"Give me a moment," Ramirez said, holding up a finger and heading into the station. He came out ten minutes later. "Sergeant and me go way back. They'll be out of your hair in five. One of them said you promised him a selfie with Mr. Nesquik? Who the heck is that?"

"Long story," I said. "Once the station is clear, get your people back and keep them back. You got EMTe on site?"

"Four blocks up on 47th," Ramirez answered. "They told me that was a good safe distance from the energy in this area."

"They would know," I said. "Once we go downstairs, this area will be locked down until we're done. No one comes in, no one goes out."

"You plan on making this mission a one-way trip?" Ramirez asked, looking at Monty and then at me. "I've never questioned your motives, just your methods. Every time, but not your dedication to keeping my city...our city, safe. Don't get dead in here. The city needs idiots like you."

He stomped off and barked orders to his people.

"Why was he staring at me when he said that last line?"

"It only means he knows you really well," Monty said, looking at his watch. "No time like the present."

"You know, Professor Ziller would argue that the present isn't really a classification of time, but rather a descriptor of a current flow state—"

"Shut it," Monty said and cracked a smile. "Ready?"

"No, but that's never stopped us before. Let's go."

We entered the station and Monty gestured. A dome of violet and blue-white energy surrounded the immediate area around the station. Monty must have seen my look of concern as I observed.

"It's called the Bulwark of Dawn," Monty said, looking at the retreating NYTF personnel vehicles. "They'll be able to leave, but once outside, they wont be able to come back in. They have ten minutes, and then everyone inside the sphere is ported out—forcibly. After that, it's keyed to Toson, Orahjene, and us."

"Ten minutes should be plenty of time for them to get clear. Let's go," I said. "We have a city to keep intact."

We headed downstairs and Monty gestured again, shunting us sideways. This Oracle room was easily five times the size of the one we visited downtown.

The confluence in the center was about twice the size of the hub at Bowling Green. This orb of energy looked like the hub of a wheel with spokes shooting off in every possible direction. The energy coming off the center orb was palpable.

"It's connected across planes, with all those extensions."

"Is that going to be a problem?"

"Only if I get it wrong," Monty said. "Then I'll have the opportunity to destroy not only this city, but multiple cities across multiple planes."

"That's not reassuring in the least," I said. "Don't get it wrong."

Monty stepped close to the confluence of energy and began gesturing. At first, nothing happened, and then I saw his symbols adhere to the orb. They attached to the extensions and began rerouting the energy in different directions, creating a loop.

Beads of sweat formed on Monty's brow. He kept

gesturing until all of the extensions formed an energetic Gordian knot, looping over and through one another. After a few more gestures, Monty stepped back and nodded.

"Not bad, if I do say so myself," he said, wiping an arm across his forehead.

"Did it work?" I asked. "That looks incredibly complicated. How are you going to unravel it?"

"We'll burn that bridge when we get to it," Monty said in his best Uncle Dex voice. "Let's go welcome our guests."

THIRTY-SEVEN

"I'm afraid we're going to have to enlist your creature to run interference with the golem again," Monty said when we reached street level. "Do you think he's up to it?"

<For extra meat, I'm up for everything.>

<Are you sure? I don't want you getting hurt.>

<I'm a hellhound. I don't get hurt, but I do starve if not fed.>

"You know the cost," I said, looking at Monty. "Extra meat."

Monty gestured and formed a sausage about the size of my leg.

"He can have that when he hits battle-mode size," Monty said. "There's five more like that one—if you stop the golem."

Peaches bowed his head and growled, a deep rumbling sound that vibrated along the ground and in the pit of my stomach. He inhaled and let out what I could only call a sonic boom of a bark. All of the ground floor windows in the surrounding buildings exploded, and several of the signs hanging directly over the station shattered, raining pieces of electrical equipment everywhere.

The runes along Peaches' flanks exploded with red light as the air around him became charged with energy. He spread his forelegs, sinking several inches into the concrete. He shook his body and barked again as his eyes gleamed red. My ears were still ringing as he grew, reaching battle-mode size. He was taller than the station as he sniffed the air.

<PREPARE, BONDMATE. A MAGE OF CONSIDERABLE POWER ARRIVES. HE BRINGS THE GOLEM.>

"Toson is on his way," I said, still in awe at Peaches' transformation. "Can we face him?"

"Together, yes," Monty said with a nod. "The Bulwark will inhibit much of the Earth's Breath's effects. The golem should be manageable for your creature now."

I looked over and saw Peaches inhaling the immense sausage Monty had created for him.

<Really? Is that all you think about?>

<THIS FORM REQUIRES SUSTENANCE, BONDMATE. I WILL BE ENGAGED IN BATTLE AND MUST MAINTAIN ENERGY LEVELS. THIS PROTEIN WILL FACILITATE MY ACTIVITY.>

<Actually, that makes perfect sense. Don't get hurt—just stop the golem.>

<THAT IS THE INTENTION. WILL YOU NEED PROTECTION?>

<I think we can handle this. If I do, I'll let you know.>

A large stone slab, easily the size of the midtown bus, sailed our way. It tumbled slowly in space as it headed lazily in our direction to crush us. Peaches turned his head and unleashed his baleful glare. Twin beams of red energy intercepted the slab and blasted it to a cloud of dust.

<Thanks. That looked like it would hurt.>

<BE CAREFUL, BONDMATE. I WILL ENGAGE THE GOLEM. BE AWARE THAT ANOTHER MAGE APPROACHES. THIS ONE GREATER IN POWER.>

"Jen is incoming," I said under my breath. "Maybe we should let them settle their differences?"

"Only if we want to call this area the crater formerly known as Times Square," Monty said, forming violet orbs of energy. "Do you still want to capture him?"

"He just tried to crush us with a boulder the size of a bus," I answered, drawing Grim Whisper. "What do you think?"

"This is not the end," Monty said, unleashing the orbs as they raced at Toson. "It is not even the beginning of the end. But it is, perhaps, the end of the beginning. Let's crush him."

"British Bulldog for the win, then," I said, firing Grim Whisper. "If you're going through hell, keep going."

I saw Peaches rush the golem, knocking it on its side. Toson screamed in anger and unleashed an orb of flame at my hellhound, who blinked out and reappeared behind Toson, unleashing his omega beams.

Toson raised a stone wall only to have it obliterated. The golem got to its feet and punched Peaches in his side, launching him across the street. Peaches shook off the blow, and then charged at the golem as Toson raced at us, hands blazing.

"Today you die," Toson said, blasting us with flame. "Today, I will scatter the ashes of your bones."

Monty raised a shield and deflected the flame to the side.

"I think he may be a bit stronger than last time," Monty said, unleashing more orbs. "His energy signature has escalated."

"Of course, I'm stronger," Toson sneered. "I deciphered the limiter you placed on my artifact and modified it. Now the golem's essence feeds me directly."

"Directly?" Monty asked, slashing a hand through the air, destroying several stone orbs headed our way. "Are you mad? Don't you know what that means?"

"It means I will have all the power," Toson boasted, raising his flame-covered arms. "I will incinerate you into ash and then I will wait for her. She will bow to me before she dies."

I pressed my mala bead, creating my shield. Monty stood next to me and reinforced it, as an enormous wall of flame headed our way.

"That looks hot, Monty. Too hot for these shields."

"I know," he said, grabbing my arm and flinging me to the side, out of the way. With another gesture he formed a blade of air, slicing his arm. I saw the blood float lazily in the air in front of him and in his hand he held the vial of *Mors Tenebris*. "I'm sorry, Simon. This is the only way to stop him."

I patted my pockets, but the box was gone.

"Monty! No!" I yelled. "That's not—"

Monty drank the vial and gestured. Nothing happened.

Toson laughed and sent more orbs of flame at Monty.

"Fool!" Toson screamed. "No one can stand against me! Burn in your death!"

<Boy, Monty needs help now!>

Two beams of red energy punched into Toson from behind, knocking him to the side. Peaches bounded forward through the wall of flame with the golem in pursuit. The golem caught up to Peaches, bringing a hammer-fist down on his back. Peaches deviated from his trajectory, slipping into a slide and crashing forward, head-first.

Monty, still in shock from the ineffective *Mors Tenebris* —actually a vial of Coke, didn't have time to get out of the way. Peaches shook his head at the last second and launched Monty to the side, away from the wall of flame. The wall of flame engulfed Peaches a second later.

"Peaches!" I screamed when he disappeared from sight. I pulled out the flask and for a split-second, I considered it, before opening the flask and pouring out the contents. I let the rage wash over me.

"Ignisvitae!" I yelled, unleashing a beam of violet energy from my hand that blasted into the golem, sending it crashing into a building. Toson looked at me in shock.

"You won't stop me," he said, running to the golem. "Your mage gave me the key. You will all die!"

The golem stood and caught the running Toson in its embrace, and the Earth's Breath exploded with orange light as Toson was absorbed into the golem. It grew taller and brighter as it stood, then looked at us and roared.

"You really should have let me drink the dark death," Monty said, looking at the Toson-golem. "He just became exponentially more lethal."

"The dark death was a horrible idea," I said, putting my flask away. "I really wish I had some coffee right about now."

The Toson-golem zeroed in on us and started running

in our direction. I felt the vibrations through the street as it closed the distance. When it was a hundred feet away, it leapt in the air, its intention to give us a flaming foot stomp of doom. Monty began gesturing and forming shields around us.

I heard the growl from behind us as Peaches bounded over us, eyes blazing, and crashed into the flaming Toson-golem. The golem grabbed Peaches and slammed him into a building before throwing him across Broadway.

Peaches shook it off, but I could tell he was out of it. He tried to walk and fell to one side.

<Stay there, boy! He'll hurt you again!>

<YOU ARE IN DANGER. YOU MUST EVACUATE THE AREA, BONDMATE.>

<Just stay there! Don't move!>

Peaches tried to stand again but fell over. The golem looked at Peaches and dismissed him with a roar as he headed our way.

"He's too strong, Monty," I said, looking at the approaching golem. "What did he do? He said you gave him the key. Which key?"

"He undid the limiter I placed on the artifact," Monty said. "By doing so, he must have found a way to merge with the artifact and the golem—creating this amalgamation of human and golem."

"That's going to come crush us."

"I think our part here is done," Monty said. "This is too much power for us."

"What are you talking about? He hurt Peaches. I'm not going to give up."

I drew Ebonsoul and approached the golem when a hand reached out and grabbed me by the shoulder.

"Simon..." Monty started.

"Let go of me, Monty," I said, shrugging off the hand. "You sit there if you want, but I'm going to go stab that bastard a few times for hurting my hellhound."

"I told you. This was my duty."

It was Jen.

THIRTY-EIGHT

It wasn't the Jen I remembered from the secret garden.

This was First Elder Orahjene in her capacity as Judge, Jury, and Executioner. She looked at me and nodded.

"Thank you both," she said, her voice slightly altered with the increased power. "This is something I must face. Something I must do."

I moved to the side as she started approaching the golem.

"That's not just the golem," I said, warning her. "Toson is in there somewhere, too."

"I know," Jen said. "If you would allow me, I have need of your hellhound."

"He's hurt," I said, looking at Peaches. "I don't think he can help you."

"He can, but first I must help him," she answered. "With your permission?"

"If it means making him better, then yes, please."

Jen waved an arm in a semi-circle, while extending the other arm in Peaches' direction. A beam of red-orange light flowed from her hand into Peaches's side. A few seconds later, the beam disappeared. Peaches got steadily to his feet and shook his body.

"Tristan, Simon, please step back," Jen said and walked forward as Peaches leapt forward and crashed into the golem, sending it tumbling. "This will be over soon."

The golem swung at Peaches, who moved back out of the way. I saw him take a breath and braced myself for one of his supersonic barks, but when he opened his mouth, a blast of red flame is what shot out, wrapping itself around the golem.

I stood there in awe as the flames kept growing over and around the golem. This wasn't normal flame.

"Hellfire," Monty said, standing next to me. "She must have helped him unlock that ability."

"Hellfire," I repeated as Peaches hit the golem with another blast. "This is going to be a problem—I think."

Jen extended both arms to the side and then moved them in a circular fashion. The energy around her body increased in intensity as she completed the circle. When her hands came together, she pushed them both forward.

The wave of energy traveling outward from Jen slammed into us and launched Monty and me down the street. After we landed, we bounced for another few feet until we finally came to a halt.

"That was unexpectedly unpleasant," Monty said with a groan. "I'd say she has definitely shifted into Archmage level, or is at the very least one shift away."

"You think?" I said. "She wasn't even trying, and we were behind her."

I looked up to see the golem gone. In it's place, stood a battered, bruised, and bloody Toson.

"Hello, Toson," Jen said. "Look at what you have done. For what? For power?"

"Jenny," Toson said through cracked lips. "I did it for us!"

"Us?" Jen said, and I felt the power spool in her direction. "You did this...for us?"

Monty gestured and cast another set of shields.

"Yes, Jenny," Toson answered. "Everything I've done... I've done for us."

"My name is not Jenny. It is O...rah...je...ne. You killed my father. Prepare to die."

"Simon, hurry," Monty said as he dropped another Bulwark dome over us.

Jen raised an arm and unleashed a beam of white light. The beam punched into Toson, obliterating him into nothing—not even dust remained. The shockwaves rushed out from her as the beam made contact and increased in intensity. Monty and I were sliding back from her as the energy dissolved Monty's shields.

I pressed my mala bead materializing my shield, only to have it disintegrate a few seconds later.

"We can't withstand too much more of this, Monty."

"I...know," he said, straining against the waves of power slamming into the Bulwark. "We're too close!"

"This is one shift away from Archmage?"

"I may have slightly miscalculated the extent of her power," Monty answered. "It would seem—"

"As First Elder," Jen's voice boomed across the area. "I, Orahjene find you, Toson of the Red Mountain sect, guilty of the crime of murder. A life for a life. Goodbye, husband."

The power threatening to wipe us out subsided almost immediately.

"Anyone worth killing is worth overkilling," I muttered to myself as I looked where Toson had once stood. "That's some serious firepower."

Monty dropped the shield, and we approached Jen. We must've looked like we'd been dragged from a warzone. Most of my clothes were wrecked. I didn't point out to Monty how shredded he appeared, because he'd already had a few bad incidents with his jackets.

"I owe you a debt I cannot repay," Jen said. "Before I go, what can I do for you?"

"What did you do to Peaches?" I asked as he bounded over, regular sized and in one piece. "Was that fire I saw come out of his mouth?"

"Hellfire," she said. "I merely nudged it forward a little. It would have manifested soon enough."

I looked around at the devastation in Times Square. I remembered what Dex had done in Japan to the damaged temple. Jen was probably just as strong as, if not stronger than Dex.

"There is one thing you could do for us," I said. "Could you handle all this damage—?"

"Simon," Monty said. "She's the First Elder of the Red Mountain, and you want her to act—"

"As a friend," Jen said, her voice holding a tinge of sadness. She formed a large orb of violet-white energy and released it into the air above us. "If you ever need my help, do not hesitate to ask. The Red Mountain is forever in your debt."

Monty placed his hands together and bowed.

Jen returned the gesture and stayed there until Monty

nudged me in the side with an elbow, reminding me to do the same. I put my hands together and bowed.

"Until our next meeting," Jen said and disappeared. "Thank you."

I looked around and Times Square was still wrecked.

"The place still looks like a warzone. Ramirez is going to have a cow. Forget that, he's going to have a herd of cows. Maybe she still doesn't have the hang of the whole First Elder thing yet?"

"Wait," Monty said. "Give it a moment."

"For what?" I asked, pointing at the orb. "I mean, sure that would be great as—I don't know? Mood lighting? It's not working as demolition repair. May as well start picking cities to move to. What do you think about Chicago?"

"They already have a wizard."

"True, but they don't have the Strong and Montague Detective Agency."

"We aren't moving," Monty said, limping away. "We'll be fine."

"I don't know how you can say that," I argued. "Once Angel sees this place, he's going to have a stroke, then kill us, and then have another stroke. This is—"

The violet-white orb above us kept rising for a few more feet. I followed it with my gaze, expecting it to float right out of the city when it exploded with a *thwump,* blinding me.

When I could see again, all of the damage was gone. I stood there turning in a circle surveying the completely undamaged Times Square.

"You better call Ramirez and tell him we're done," Monty said as he limped around the corner onto 6th

Avenue. "Tell him the city is safe—again. At least for today."

"How did she do that?" I asked, catching up. "Wait, the hub. Is Ursula going to come hunt us down when she discovers what—?"

"The permutational persistence will have run its sequence by now," Monty answered. "It will revert back to normal."

"Which means it's not hammertime?"

"Exactly," Monty said. "I need a hot shower, a hot cuppa, and perhaps two to three days of uninterrupted sleep."

"That sounds like an excellent plan—if you just adjust that cuppa for coffee, it would be perfect. I have to make one stop before I sleep for a week. Did you still want your laxative cookies?"

"Digestives—McVities, and get me three boxes, not two."

"McVittles, got it," I said. "Sounds like dog food, but okay."

He shook his head, opened a portal and vanished from sight.

I stepped into a bookstore across the street from the Library, and grabbed some books, before heading downtown. I arrived at the Bowling Green hub and parked behind Ursula's Widow. I pressed a finger on her car, leaving a fairly large smudge on the immaculate wax job before stepping into the Oracle.

"He did it anyway, didn't he?" she asked. "Even after I told him not to?"

"He's not big on following orders," I said. "I brought you this because you've had a deprived childhood."

I passed her a large box.

She opened it and gave me a small smile.

"Thanks," she said, placing the box carefully to one side. "Where do I start?"

"You start with *The Hobbit*, then move on to *The Fellowship of the Ring*. Make sure you call me when you get to Gandalf's best part."

"Will do," Ursula said as I turned to head out of the Oracle. "Where are you headed?"

"I have to go get some laxative cookies for Monty, and then I'm going to swing by the place and get my favorite hellhound"—I rubbed Peaches behind the ear—"some pastrami. Maybe have a chat with Ezra."

<I'm your only hellhound.>

<That's why you're my favorite.>

<The angry man owes me meat.>

<We'll get some at the place.>

<I would like that. Can I have extra for the beautiful guardian?>

<Let's discuss it when we get there. I think there may be some lizard conditions.>

"You do realize who Ezra is...right?" Ursula asked. "Capital D?"

"Like Monty said...in the end, we all sit at his table. I'm just doing it now, while I can still enjoy it."

I left the Oracle, jumped behind the wheel of the Dark Goat after the Sprawlmeister got comfortable in the backseat, roared the engine a few times, and headed uptown.

THE END

AUTHOR NOTES

Thank you for reading this story and jumping back into the Monty & Strong World.

Writing this story (even in the midst of con-crud) was a great adventure. Hopefully by this point you've read the book, if not go back to the beginning—here be **SPOILERS.**

It was exciting to see the development of MS&P along with Cece and other assorted characters. Yes, we will see more of the young Jotnar ice mage in future MS&P stories as well as the Brew & Chew where she, Peaches, Rags, and Frank wreak havoc on an unsuspecting city, all while saving it. Hey, they had great teachers in the wreaking havoc department.

Peaches gets HELLFIRE in XL battle-mode! WHOA!

Felt like that needed its own space there. Peaches is growing and evolving(and negotiating...anyone want to form a Hellhound Onion?) along with Simon. This story is setting the foundation for what starts happening in the next few M&S books. Monty was willing to take the Dark

Death, while Simon rejected the allure of power. The Dark Council has unofficially declared MS&P targets and placed them on a Kill On Sight list, which will make their difficult lives a bit tougher. In addition to all of that, there are forces from Simon's past that remember...and plan to remind him. Painfully and violently.

I'm really excited to reveal what's coming in the MS World in the next books, but Peaches just growled at me and promised to remove one of my arms if I did. I need my arms, so I will refrain...for now.

Even though there was a bit of destruction in this story, it couldn't be permanent. Even M&S know better than to destroy Times Square if they want to continue living in the city. Another factor for the lack of destruction is that their past is slowly catching up with them. There is plenty of destruction that has gone unanswered, and those accounts are coming due...can anyone say Archmage Julien and The Hybrid?

On the subject of Chi, we don't know where she is... yet. What we do know is that there are factions within the Dark Council that want MS&P eliminated, will do everything to remove her from power, and are willing to plunge the Council into a civil war.

That will all be explored in a story of her own titled: **BLOOD ASCENSION-RULE OF THE COUNCIL**, which will be the first of three stories culminating in her return, and facing off against the forces of the Dark Council. Michiko will do everything in her power to prevent the destruction of the Dark Council, but the cost she eventually ends up paying may be an ultimate one...we'll see.

With each book, I want to introduce you to different

elements of the world Monty & Strong inhabit, slowly revealing who they are and why they make the choices they do. Along with this, I hope to show how they are evolving and coming to terms to the changes in their lives. Simon, at some point has to accept he isn't entirely human anymore. Monty must deal with the allure of dark magic, and Peaches...well, a hellhound has to deal with getting enough meat, because we all know...Meat is...you know the rest.

Many times you will feel like Simon, a little out of your depth. We've all been there. Some of us visit that state daily. The state of confusion, uncertainty, or insecurity. He hides it well with his snark, but behind the sarcasm is— fear. The fear he will lose his family and all he holds dear and precious. There is also the fear of losing himself. He has seen what power can do—he doesn't want to go down that path. The dilemma he faces is...he may not have a choice.

This situation is intentional, because we've all been where Simon finds himself. We've all had experiences where we didn't know what was going on. Simon lives that everyday. He deals with it by being a smart ass and occasionally speaking before he thinks, except now, he's realizing that with great power, comes great coffee—and stronger enemies willing to erase you from existence.

This is currently **BOOK TEN** of the M&S series... WOW! I never imagined when I wrote *Tombyards & Butterflies* three years ago (Feb 2017) that I would still be jumping into adventures with them three years later. I owe that to you...THANK YOU! Here's to many more years of MS&P!

If you want to know how Monty & Simon met, that

story is told in a short titled: **NO GOD IS SAFE**, which explains how Tristan and Simon worked their first case, and how Simon became a cursed immortal. It wasn't due to his great charm...trust me.

There are some references you will understand and some...you may not. This may be attributable to my advanced age, (I'm older than Monty, or feel that way most mornings) or my love of all things sci-fi, fantasy, cyberpunk, Whovian, and other assorted realms I visit in my life.

As a reader, I've always enjoyed finding these "Easter Eggs" in the books I read. I hope you do too. These references occur spontaneously and I barely have control of where they will pop up. Simon is an avid Star Wars fan, while Monty prefers the cerebral Star Trek, for example. If there is a reference you don't understand, feel free to email me, and I will explain it...maybe. Bribing with large amounts Deathwish coffee and chocolate has been known to work wonders.

Simon is slowly wrapping his head around the world of magic and his role in it, but it's a vast universe, and he has no map. Bear with him—he's still new to the immortal, magical world he's been delicately shoved into. Fortunately, he has Monty, Peaches, Dex, LD, TK, and Chi (to name a few) to nudge (or blast) him in the right direction. Each book will reveal more about their backgrounds and lives before they met. Rather than hit you with a whole history, I want you to learn about them slowly, the way we do with a person we just met—over time (and many, many large cups of Deathwish Coffee).

Thank you for taking the time to read this book. I wrote it for you and I hope you enjoyed spending a few hours getting in (and out of) trouble with the Trio of Terror. If you enjoyed this story— **Please leave a review**. It's really important and helps the book (and me).

Plus, it means Peaches gets a new reinforced titanium bowl (he keeps chewing through them), industrial strength chew toys, and can get some extra sausage to impress Rags with. This will keep my shoes, assorted furniture, my arms and legs from random hellhound shredding.

Also, I get to keep him at normal size (most of the time). There is no way I could house a Peaches XL without the National Guard paying me a visit to intervene. They tend to frown upon extra large hellhounds running around the city. Who knew?

Thank you again for jumping into this adventure with me.

SPECIAL MENTIONS

Larry & Tammy—The WOUF: Because even when you aren't there...you're there.

Tammy: Because anything worth killing is worth overkilling.

Jim Z: For refractory casting that bends light around an object and is the basis for Simon's first defensive spell —Camouflage.

Jim Z: for the monocle...get out of my head.

Luann & Diviana: For being even more amazing in real life than you are in this book. Keep making your mom proud and focus on being a better person each day. Luann, making the request puts you squarely in the awesome mom category. It was my honor and privilege.

Orlando A. Sanchez

www.orlandoasanchez.com

Orlando has been writing ever since his teens when he was immersed in creating scenarios for playing Dungeon and Dragons with his friends every weekend.

The worlds of his books are urban settings with a twist of the paranormal lurking just behind the scenes and generous doses of magic, martial arts, and mayhem.

He currently resides in Queens, NY with his wife and children.

BITTEN PEACHES PUBLISHING

Thanks for Reading

If you enjoyed this book, would you please **leave a review**
at the site you purchased it from? It doesn't have to be
long... just a line or two would be fantastic and it would
really help me out.

Bitten Peaches Publishing offers more books by this
author. From science fiction & fantasy to adventure &
mystery, we bring the best stories for adults and kids alike.

www.BittenPeachesPublishing.com

More books by Orlando A. Sanchez

The Warriors of the Way

The Karashihan*•The Spiritual Warriors•The
Ascendants•The Fallen Warrior•The Warrior
Ascendant•TheMaster Warrior

The Birth of Death

Gideon Shepherd Thrillers
Sheepdog

DAMNED
Aftermath

*Books denoted with an asterisk are **FREE** via my website—www.orlandoasanchez.com

ACKNOWLEDEGEMENTS

With each book, I realize that every time I learn something about this craft, it highlights so many things I still have to learn. Each book, each creative expression, has a large group of people behind it.

This book is no different.

Even though you see one name on the cover, it is with the knowledge that I am standing on the shoulders of the literary giants that informed my youth, and am supported by my generous readers who give of their time to jump into the adventures of my overactive imagination.

I would like to take a moment to express my most sincere thanks:

To Dolly: my wife and greatest support. You make all this possible each and everyday. You keep me grounded when I get lost in the forest of ideas. Thank you for asking the right questions when needed, and listening intently when I go off on tangents. Thank you for who you are and the space you create—I love you.

To my Tribe: You are the reason I have stories to tell. You cannot possibly fathom how much and how deeply I love you all.

To Lee: Because you were the first audience I ever had. I love you sis.

To the Logsdon Family: The words, *thank you* are insufficient to describe the gratitude in my heart for each of you. JL your support always demands I bring my best, my A-game, and produce the best story I can. Both you and Lorelei(my Uber Jeditor) and now, Audrey, are the reason I am where I am today. My thank you for the notes, challenges, corrections, advice, and laughter. Your patience is truly infinite. *Arigatogozaimasu.*

To The Montague & Strong Case Files Group-AKA The MoB (Mages of Badassery): When I wrote T&B there were fifty-five members in The MoB. As of this release there are over one-thousand members in the MoB. I am honored to be able to call you my MoB Family. Thank you for being part of this group and M&S. You make this possible. **THANK YOU.**

To the WTA-The Incorrigibles: JL, Ben Z. Eric QK., and S.S.

They sound like a bunch of badass misfits, because they are. My exposure to the deranged and deviant brain trust you all represent helped me be the author I am today. I have officially gone to the *dark side* thanks to all of you. I humbly give you my thanks, and...it's all your fault.

To my fellow Indie Authors, specifically the tribe at 20books to 50k: Thank you for creating a space where authors can feel listened to, and encouraged to continue on this path. A rising tide lifts all the ships indeed.

To The English Advisory: Aaron, Penny, Carrie and all of the UK MoB. For all things English...thank you.

To DEATH WISH COFFEE: This book (and every book I write) has been fueled by generous amounts of the only coffee on the planet (and in space) strong enough to power my very twisted imagination. Is there any other coffee that can compare? I think not. DEATHWISH-thank you!

To Deranged Doctor Design: Kim, Darja, Tanja, and Milo.

If you've seen the covers of my books and been amazed, you can thank the very talented and gifted creative team at DDD. They take the rough ideas I give them, and produce incredible covers that continue to surprise and amaze me. Each time, I find myself striving to write a story worthy of the covers they produce. DDD you embody professionalism and creativity. Thank you for the great service and spectacular covers. **YOU GUYS RULE!**

To you, the reader: I was always taught to save the best for last. I write these stories for you. Thank you for jumping down the rabbit holes of *what if?* with me. You are the reason I write the stories I do.

You keep reading...I'll keep writing.

Thank you for your support and encouragement.

CONTACT ME

I really do appreciate your feedback. You can let me know what you thought of the story by emailing me at:
orlando@orlandoasanchez.com

To get **FREE** stories please visit my page at:
www.orlandoasanchez.com

For more information on the M&S World...come join the MoB Family on Facebook!
You can find us at:
Montague & Strong Case Files

If you enjoyed the book, **please leave a review**. They help the book and other readers find good stories to read.
THANK YOU!

ART SHREDDERS

No book is the work of one person. I am fortunate enough to have an amazing team of advance readers and shredders. They give their time and keen eyes to provide notes, insight, and corrections (dealing wonderfully with my dreaded comma allergy). They help make every book and story go from good to great. Each and every one of you helped make this book fantastic.

THANK YOU

ART SHREDDERS

Alisia Soles, Anne Morando, Audra Vroman Meyers, Audra Cienki,

Barbara Hamm, Barbara Henninger, Bennah Phelps, Beverly Collie, Brandy Dalton, Brenda Nix Lively, Brett Wickersham,

Cam Skaggs, Carolyn Christiansen, Carrie Anne

O'Leary, Cat Inglis, Chris Christman II, Colleen Taylor, Connor Jarczynski,

Dana Audette, Darren Musson, Davina Noble, Dawn McQueen Mortimer, Denise King, Diana Gray, Diane Kassman, Dolly Sanchez, Donna Young Hatridge, Dorothy MPG,

Hal Bass, Helen Gibson,

Jim Stoltz, Jen Cooper, Jeremy Jarczynski, Joscelyn Smith, Joy Ollier, Julie Peckett,

Karen Hollyhead, Karen Langan, Kyle Rodenbeck,

Larry Diaz Tushman, Laura Tallman I, LeAnne Benson, Lesley Sharp, Luann Zip,

Malcolm Robertson, Marcia Campbell, Maryelaine Eckerle-Foster, Melissa Miller, Melody DeLoach, Mike Helas,

Natalie Fallon, Nick Church,

Penny Haller, Penny Campbell-Myhill,

RC Battels, Rene Corrie, Rob Hill,

Sara Mason Branson, Sean Trout, Shanon Owens Bainbridge, Sharon Harradine, Shelley Sears, Sondra Massey, Stacey Stein, Stephanie Claypoole,

Tami Cowles, Tanya Anderson, Ted Camer, Terri Adkisson, Thomas Ryan, Tommy Owens,

Vikki Brannagan,

Wanda Corder-Jones, Wendy Schindler,

Zak Klepek.

Thanks for Reading
If you enjoyed this book, would you **please leave a review** at the site you purchased it from? It doesn't have to be a book report... just a line or two would be fantastic and it would really help us out!

Made in the USA
Middletown, DE
20 January 2020